"Matt, is this my room or yours?"

"Ours, I gather. Your friend Adrian Banks booked it." Matt moved intimidatingly close. "Don't pretend you're surprised, Pippa."

"Of course I'm surprised!" Pippa burst out angrily. "I'd never intended to share a room with Adrian, and he knew it!"

Matt's smile relayed disbelief. "Do I take it, then, that you wouldn't consider sharing a room with me?"

"Of course I wouldn't!" Pippa's eyes flashed fire. "And unless you start treating me with some respect, I'll leave Tokyo tonight!"

Surprisingly, Matt laughed. "Oh, I do like you when you're angry!"

"You've been baiting me, you beast!"

"Pippa, I needed to find out what was under that attractive exterior." Matt's tone was solemn again.

"Well, I'd be fascinated to hear your conclusions," she responded caustically.

"Then here's one—Adrian Banks isn't the man for you."

Marjorie Lewty is a born romantic. "It's all in the way you look at the world," she suggests. "Maybe if I hadn't been lucky enough to find love myself—in my parents, my husband, my children—I might have viewed the world with cynicism." As it is, she writes about "what is surely the most important and exciting part of growing up, and that is falling in love." She and her family live in Leamington, a pleasant town full of beautiful parks and old Georgian homes.

Books by Marjorie Lewty

HARLEQUIN ROMANCE

2282—A VERY SPECIAL MAN
2331—A CERTAIN SMILE
2382—PRISONER IN PARADISE
2421—LOVE IS A DANGEROUS GAME
2450—BEYOND THE LAGOON
2498—A GIRL BEWITCHED
2546—MAKESHIFT MARRIAGE
2579—ONE WHO KISSES
2587—DANGEROUS MALE
2650—RIVIERA ROMANCE
2678—LOVERS' KNOT
2746—A LAKE IN KYOTO

HARLEQUIN PRESENTS

875—ACAPULCO MOONLIGHT
932—VILLA IN THE SUN

Don't miss any of our special offers. Write to us at the following address for information on our newest releases.

Harlequin Reader Service
901 Fuhrmann Blvd., P.O. Box 1397, Buffalo, NY 14240
Canadian address: P.O. Box 603,
Fort Erie, Ont. L2A 5X3

In Love with the Man

Marjorie Lewty

Harlequin Books

TORONTO • NEW YORK • LONDON
AMSTERDAM • PARIS • SYDNEY • HAMBURG
STOCKHOLM • ATHENS • TOKYO • MILAN

Original hardcover edition published in 1986
by Mills & Boon Limited

ISBN 0-373-02848-2

Harlequin Romance first edition July 1987

CHAPTER ONE

'ALL ready for take-off tomorrow, Pippa? Looking forward to the trip to the mysterious Orient?'

The pale blue eyes of the thin young man at the computer table twinkled teasingly behind his large spectacles, but he didn't move them from the screen of the VDU in front of him.

Philippa Marsden perched on the edge of her own table, where everything had been cleared away twenty minutes ago, swinging her long, nicely curved legs impatiently as she stared down through the window of the first-floor office. What she saw below was mostly the wide expanse of grass that graced the front of the old manor house between Warwick and Kenilworth, which was now the Systems and Research Branch of a huge engineering corporation with headquarters in Birmingham. But if she stretched her neck she could just see the corner of the staff car-park round the side of the house. Staff were leaving, cars were starting up and trickling away towards the gates, down there behind a bank of trees. Was Adrian's red Volvo still in the car-park? She couldn't see it.

Come on, come *on*, Sam, she willed the bespectacled young man silently. Finish. Pack up and let's get off. Because if she didn't get away very soon she would miss the chance of a lift home to Warwick in Adrian's car. She had left her own car at the garage yesterday to be serviced and resprayed while she was away on the Tokyo trip.

5

The Tokyo trip! Excitement stirred inside her every time she thought about it, although she had known for nearly three weeks that she had been chosen to be one of the team to go to Japan on a fact-finding mission for the company.

She had always longed to travel, and now just saying the word 'Tokyo' to herself brought a brighter sparkle to her large dark blue eyes. Just imagining herself in the huge Oriental city she had read so much about, where East and West join in a marvellous coloured kaleidoscope! And imagining Adrian there to share it all with her. Heaven!

'I'm thrilled, Sam,' she said, 'you know I am.' 'But——' she gazed across the office that had once been a gracious bedroom, and now bristled with computers and visual display units and all the other electronic gear of a later age, and added slowly and pointedly, '*But* I've still got my packing to do—and lots of other oddments.' Like washing her hair and trying that new conditioner that was supposed to lift its red-gold colour with fascinating lights. Like leaving her room clean and tidy, so that Mrs Smithson didn't have anything to do there while Philippa was away. Like finishing the report that she'd been working on for a week, and with which she was going to surprise and please Adrian. Like— oh, a dozen other things.

'O.K., love.' Sam Gunner frowned into the small screen before him and touched a couple of keys, then frowned again as the pattern of lists on the screen changed. 'Give me another five minutes.'

Philippa sighed and looked at her watch. 'Not a minute more,' she said. She went on peering out of the window. More cars were leaving now, but she thought she could pick out Adrian's red Volvo among the stationary ones. She might yet catch him. If not—well, she would just have to wait for a bus, which would be a nuisance because it was beginning to rain and the late afternoon buses from Stratford were often full by the time they reached here.

That was one of the penalties of working in the country. You needed transport, and the monthly payments on her car ate into her salary. But she loved her job and knew she was making a success of it. Sam had been very encouraging lately. All the same she still had to pinch herself to believe that she was going to Japan tomorrow.

Adrian himself had told her a fortnight ago. 'Drop in at my office this afternoon around three,' he had said. Philippa had been going off for lunch and they had met in the imposing entrance hall that had once hung with banners and shields and portraits of ancestors, and was now painted flat cream and adorned with one or two large modern abstract paintings.

The sun had been shining through the long stained-glass window on Adrian's crisp fair hair and sun-bronzed face, and she had thought suddenly what a good-looking, attractive man he was. She had only encountered him once or twice since he joined the staff at the branch, and had never actually spoken to him, and when he stopped and said, 'Hullo, Miss Marsden, I've been looking for you. I've got a proposition to put to you,' she could hardly believe her ears.

He had smiled into her eyes, making a joke of his questionable choice of words, and—after a split second's hesitation—Philippa had smiled back. The word 'proposition' had overtones that she was wary about, but Adrian Banks was the branch's public relations manager and this proposition must be a business one.

That was exactly what it was. In his office, that afternoon, he had smiled across his imposing desk at her and said, 'How would you feel about joining my team for Tokyo, Miss Marsden?'

If she hadn't been sitting down her legs would have buckled up under her. 'Me?' she gasped. 'Why me?'

Adrian sat back, still smiling. He had an intriguing smile, a mischievous, little-boy smile that disarmed you. 'Why not? Sam seems to think a lot of your work. Says you're as good, or better, than Rex. We need a fourth in the team and who more suitable than Philippa Marsden? I'm sure, too, that our Japanese friends will appreciate meeting such an extremely attractive young lady. Well, what do you say?'

'I say yes,' said Philippa promptly. 'And thank you for including me.'

'The pleasure is mine.' He stood up and came round the desk. 'Tokyo's a fascinating place. We can hit some of the high spots when the day's grind is over.' He put a hand lightly on her shoulder. 'Suppose you have dinner with me tonight and we talk about the trip?'

Less than three weeks ago, and yet it seemed now that she had known Adrian for years. That first dinner had been followed by two more in the next weeks. Adrian seemed to value her company; it wasn't long since he had been transferred from Head Office in Birmingham and he knew nobody in this part of the world, he told Philippa. He was living at the Lord Leycester Hotel in Warwick until he found a house or a flat for himself.

They got on famously together. Adrian wanted to know all about Philippa—where she lived, her family. She turned the questions off, as she always did. She didn't talk about her father—or her mother. Strangers took it for granted that she had lost them both, and in a way she had. But she did talk about the cottage out in the country where she had lived with her grandmother. 'She was a darling. So young for her age—such fun. She died three months ago.' She was silent, looking away, biting her lip. Adrian squeezed her hand in sympathy and she warmed towards him. Not everyone took the death of a grandmother very seriously, but she thought he knew how she felt. Perhaps he had a beloved grandmother himself.

After a little silence he said, 'So now you're on your own?'

Philippa nodded. 'We sold Gran's cottage and I'm living with Mr and Mrs Smithson, friends of Gran's, until I find a flat.'

'We must go flat-hunting together after Tokyo,' Adrian said. 'You never know—we might decide to share one.'

He wasn't serious, of course, and they laughed together, but there was something in his voice, in the way he looked at her——

'You're quite a girl, aren't you, Philippa? If it weren't a sexist statement I'd say you're much too pretty to be a computer boffin.'

She had a dimple in her left cheek when she smiled. 'Oh, boffins come in all shapes and sizes these days. Actually, I'm only half a boffin as yet. I make the coffee for Sam and Rex and listen to their moans when their programs have "bugs" in them and pick up the seas of waste paper they throw around.'

'I thought the idea of high-tech was a paperless office?' Adrian raised a humorously wry eyebrow.

'H'm, that's a thought, it *is*. But you need reams of paper to plan out how you arrive at a paperless office. Funny, when you come to think of it.' It seemed funnier than it really was and they laughed about it for quite a time. They were dining at Adrian's hotel and Philippa had an idea that he had been filling up her wine glass rather too enthusiastically.

'And what else do you do in this temple of high technology besides making the coffee?'

She didn't want to go on an ego-trip, although she knew that her work was becoming increasingly important to Sam and Rex. 'Oh, I help out here and there. They give me subs to work on. And I check the data-codes and so on.'

He spread out his hands helplessly. 'Subs? Codes? It's all as clear as mud.'

'But surely you know about computing?'

'Not a lot—yet,' Adrian confessed 'I'm only a humble PR man, you know, but I mean to learn the jargon fast.' He filled up her wine glass again. 'Perhaps you'd like to teach me? Tell me, how did you come to take this up?'

Philippa shrugged. 'They put me into the computer studies class at school. There were too many boys in it and I think they wanted to even things out so that the class wouldn't look sexist. It sort of—took with me.'

Adrian regarded her with admiration across the table. In the light from the candles his warm brown eyes, smiling into hers, gave her a little thrill of excitement. 'I'll say it did. Bright girl!'

'You don't have to be all that bright, hard work mostly.'

'And a logical mind. I see I shall have to treat you with great caution.'

Philippa laughed. She had a delightful laugh, low and husky, and two men at the next table looked their way with interest. 'Oh, please don't feel you must do that,' she said.

Adrian stretched across the table and covered her hand with his. 'I hope that means what I want it to mean,' he said, smiling.

She gave him a demure glance. She had a heady feeling that she was at the beginning of something important in her life. She hadn't felt like this since Gerald, but she didn't want to remember that.

And the first change was the week in Tokyo—in Adrian's team. She just couldn't wait.

There had been a good deal to do in her spare time. On Saturday she went on a shopping spree at the big Leamington stores, and spent a week's wages on two light dresses, and all the accessories she thought she might need. Adrian had told her that the weather in Tokyo should be beautiful in April. The cherry blossom was quite something, he said. They must go on a trip outside the city to see it. He had been to Japan before and knew all the best places. He lent her a Tokyo guide-book and she pored over it, reading about the fantastic sights and sounds of the second largest and most colourful city in the world. For a fortnight she lived, slept and dreamed Tokyo.

And with Adrian beside her to enjoy it all with! It was almost too good to be true.

But it *was* true, and tomorrow they would leave—the four of them: Adrian, who would lead the team and do all the public relations work, booking hotels, arranging transport and meetings with Japanese firms; Sam and Rex, who were the technical specialists and herself. She still wasn't quite sure what her own role would be, but she was happy to wait until Adrian told her. Adrian! He really was rather special.

She was brought back to earth now as Sam erupted with annoyance on the other side of the office.

'Damn!' He ran frantic fingers through untidy brown hair. 'This blasted program's got a jinx on it.' He pointed an accusing finger at the small screen in front of him, covered with lines and figures. 'Will it run? No, it won't.'

Philippa sighed and glanced at her wristwatch. Sam Gunner's dedication to his computer was a byword in the branch and once he got his teeth into a new program he lost all sense of time.

'Five minutes up,' she said.

Sam got the message this time. He sat back, pushed his spectacles up his nose and grinned across at her. 'O.K., Pippa, you win. Might as well pack it in now, anyway. No hope of getting this program working before we leave.' He extracted the disk and switched the computer off; tore a wad of sheets from his scratch-pad and aimed them at the waste-basket. 'We'll pack up and get along, then. O.K.?'

'Fine.' Relieved, Philippa stooped to retrieve the screwed-up ball of paper which had missed its target, and Sam found his eyes lingering on the slim form in the swingy grey skirt and white blouse. It was rare for Sam's short-sighted eyes to focus for long on anything except his VDU, but Pippa Marsden was certainly worth looking at. Super legs, curves in the right places, gorgeous copper-coloured hair that swung into her neck like one of those telly ads, and a creamy smile that could turn a fellow on—if he was ready to be turned on, which Sam wasn't. Yes, thought Sam, almost regretfully, if he had been into girls himself, instead of into computers, then Pippa Marsden would be the one he would go for. Not that he would get very far with her. He had seen the way she looked at that Adrian Banks fellow who had taken over the PR department. Showy devil, with his crinkly hair and his sun-bed tan and his pong of aftershave. Sam didn't like the type; he hoped Pippa knew what she was doing. Probably did—Pippa had a cool way with her when something or someone didn't please her. The best kind of modern girl, Pippa. Bright, too. Very bright. Good at her job.

Sam was no sexist. Pippa knew her way round a computer as well as any of the assistants he had had working for him at different times, and when they got back from Tokyo he planned to try her out on some of the more complicated programming. There were new ideas in the wind, exciting ideas. Things were hotting up in the department and he and Rex had their hands pretty full already.

Oblivious to the fact that she was the object of Sam's musings, Philippa extracted the afternoon's crop of waste paper from the basket and fed it into the shredder, watching the little ribbons of paper issuing from the machine. Part of her own job in the department was to make sure that every bit of scrap paper was shredded. Sam said that nobody would be likely to extract much joy from his scribbles, but Philippa thought she saw the point of the exercise. It was in this department that all new ideas were worked on, and in the world of engineering high technology new ideas were more precious than gold.

Sometimes, if she happened to wake in the night, she had awful visions of silent-footed thieves creeping in, wearing black stocking masks, shining torch beams around in the darkness, and coming across a piece of scrap paper she had missed, one with an important data code on it, perhaps. If they knew the code-words that protected the program data-files they could break into Sam's confidential program. She knew it happened. It was common knowledge that some large companies and banks lost millions of pounds a year because of computer thieves—hackers, they called them.

Sam began to pack his own gear and sighed. 'Personally, I'm not exactly yearning for a week in Tokyo myself. I'd rather stay here and get this blasted program running. What's the good of having a brilliant ideas man like Matt Vane in charge here if you can't deliver the goods? Like asking Prost or Andretti to drive a Formula One car round Brands Hatch when the mechanics can't get the gears to function.'

Philippa switched off the shredder and said idly, '*Is* our Mr Vane all that brilliant?' Matthew Vane had come from Head Office in Birmingham recently to take charge of the branch, when the previous director was transferred to London.

'Brilliant? I'll say he is! I.Q. up in the top two per cent. Super chap to work for, too.' Sam's pale blue eyes behind the large spectacles glowed with enthusiasm.

Philippa hadn't had any contact with the new head of the branch, except for a brief introductory session for all the staff when he first arrived. What she had seen of him she certainly didn't take to. She had to admit to prejudice, but the fact was that he reminded her of Gerald—the same tall, dark good looks, the same charisma, so sure of himself and his ability to make everyone see things his way. After the painful, jagged break with Gerald that had left a nasty void in her life for nearly a year, it was to pleasant, easy, fairish men that Philippa had turned. Men like Adrian Banks.

'If Matthew Vane's all that brilliant I wonder why he moved out here,' she said. 'Perhaps he fancied country life. Sees himself as the squire—living here in a luxury penthouse at the top of the Manor.'

Sam crammed the final notebook into his bulging holdall and shot her a keen glance. 'I take it you haven't joined the Matt Vane fan club then?'

'Me?' Philippa hooted with laughter. 'Never!'

'Sexy?' suggested Sam mischievously.

'Maybe, if you like the macho type—all dark, smouldering good looks, and arrogant with it. No, thank you!' Adrian was slim, with sun-bleached streaks in his hair, and laughing brown eyes and a smile that made Philippa smile back.

She picked up her bag and walked towards the door. Thank goodness Sam seemed ready to leave at last. It was a rule that nobody should be left on their own in the 'confidential' office.

But before she could open the door it was pushed forcefully from the outside and Matthew Vane appeared in the doorway. He seemed to Philippa almost to fill it with his impressive size. He wore the casual clothes that all the men wore in the research department—except Adrian, who had dealings with customers and dressed more formally. But Matthew Vane's casual clothes were a cut above all the others. His black crew neck sweater was surely pure cashmere and it sat smoothly over shoulders that would have been useful on a rugger field; his jeans were of the expensive stretch variety and fitted without a crease over slim, muscular thighs and long legs. A slim gold watch glittered at his wrist, and the thin gold chain he wore only seemed to accentuate his masculinity. Beastly show-off, thought Philippa, hiding from herself the fact that she couldn't help being ever so slightly impressed by the man.

Sam didn't exactly jump to attention, but Philippa felt he had an urge to. Matthew Vane was a leader, it was built into every line of his hard, self-contained face. He was the kind who demands loyalty from those who work under him, and expects instant obedience. Philippa was glad that she wasn't one of them.

He stood in the doorway looking over the office and its two occupants with a sweep of keen, heavily lashed grey eyes.

'You two finished? I'd like you both up in my flat straight away. Briefing for the journey tomorrow. Is Rex around? Bring him along too.'

He nodded and withdrew. High-handed, thought Philippa. Typical! And once again she was glad she didn't have to work for him if he always issued orders in that curt fashion. But if there were to be a briefing session, then Adrian would be there and she could ask him for a lift home.

'Well, off we go then, at our master's command,'

grinned Sam, without rancour. 'Where's Rex—have you seen him lately? He's probably skived off to have a smoke.'

Philippa went to the window again and looked down. From the car-park there was a drive leading towards the gates, and narrower paths curving round to the various entrances to the house. Along one of these paths Philippa saw Rex Hanling, the third member of their department, approaching the house from the direction of the car-park, drawing on a cigarette. He walked slowly, head bent as if deep in thought.

Sam looked over her shoulder, 'There he is, smoking like a chimney, as usual, the idiot!' He clucked impatiently. 'Can't give it up, can he?' He threw open the window and bawled down, 'Hey, Rex—you're wanted up here!'

Rex looked up. He was a thin man, fortyish, with a clever, pale face, and seen from up here the balding patch on top of his head was very noticeable. Like Sam he was an expert hi-tech operator, but somehow Philippa had never seen in him the dedication that Sam showed in every possible way.

Rex hesitated, then stubbed out his cigarette and stuck it into the pocket of his jacket. 'Coming!' he shouted back, and quickened his pace to a trot.

A minute or two later he arrived in the office, breathing quickly.

'The boss wants us all up in his flat—he'll be hopping mad if he's kept waiting,' Sam told him.

'Oh lor',' mumbled Rex. 'I just nipped out for a smoke.'

Sam raised his eyebrows but made no comment, and the three of them filed out of the office and Sam locked the door behind them.

A door on the landing opened on to a narrow staircase that led up to the penthouse flat on the top floor of the old house, the part that once had been servants' quarters. The main staircase of the house was wide, its curved balustrade intricately carved, but up here the servants had had to put up with something far more modest. It was odd, Philippa thought, how the thick chocolate-brown carpet on the stairs, the matt-papered cream walls with small old maps hung at intervals, transformed the narrow wooden stairway; seemed to proclaim, 'Up these stairs you come to a place of unique importance where you will encounter power, influence, a man to be reckoned with.' Philippa had never been up here before, and she was surprised by the odd little quirk of apprehension that gripped her inside as she followed Sam up the stairs, with Rex tagging on behind, their feet sinking into the luxurious depth of the carpet.

The door on the landing at the top of the stairs was of old, stripped wood, with a solid brass knocker. All of a piece, Philippa thought; designed to impress. Well, she was not disposed to be impressed; all she wanted was to make sure that Adrian was here, behind that door. She would feel much more comfortable in Matthew Vane's presence if Adrian were beside her.

The door opened abruptly to Sam's knock and Matthew Vane himself led the way into what was evidently his living-room. Architects must have been busy here, knocking down walls, turning small rooms into this one long, gracious room with wide windows overlooking the green of trees and grass below. Thick black beams ran at odd angles across the low ceiling and down the walls, dividing the room into nooks and crannies. The furniture was cleverly arranged to leave wide empty spaces of brown carpet. There were plump sofas and chairs in pale leather, low tables, a writing-desk, a smoked-glass drinks wagon, a collection of *objets d'art* on shelves tucked away in alcoves. An elegant room, just what you'd expect for a high-powered executive. Philippa preferred something more cosy.

Matthew Vane strolled across to the drinks wagon. 'We're all here, then. Sit down, what'll you drink? Sam? Rex? Miss Marsden?' He glanced over his shoulder casually.

All here? Where was Adrian, then? Philippa's eyes moved restlessly round the room as if he could somehow have got in without her seeing him. Then she relaxed. Of course, as head of the team Adrian would have been briefed first, probably earlier on this afternoon. He might even have left already. Her heart sank. No lift home for her today, then. Still, with a whole week of Adrian's company, starting tomorrow, to look forward to, what did a few minutes in his car matter?

'Miss Marsden?' Matthew Vane's voice from above her head made her jump.

'Yes?' she murmured.

'I asked you what you'd have to drink,' he said, underlining the words patiently.

'Oh—er—sherry, please. Dry,' she added because that sounded more sophisticated. It was silly, but this room had that effect on her. It was a— a *diminishing* kind of room, unless you were very, very sure of yourself. In normal circumstances

Philippa was reasonably happy about her poise, but
something about this place unsettled her.

Matthew Vane loomed above her, holding out a
glass. 'Thank you.' She tried to look self-possessed
and nonchalant, but the big squashy chair swallowed
her up and she was afraid if she leaned back she
would spill her sherry. She sipped the drink and
glanced up at Matthew Vane, but he had already
moved away and was standing with his back to the
inglenook fireplace, whisky glass in hand, surveying
the three sitting before him. Like a Victorian father
lecturing his family, thought Philippa, disliking
him.

He raised his glass. 'Here's to the success of the
trip,' he said. 'The trade fair should be particularly
interesting to Sam and Rex—I expect you two will
spend most of your time there. And there are
arrangements to take you over one of their engineering plants, which is very much in our line. They
probably have things to teach us but we can undoubt-
edly bring a few new ideas to them. It's possible that
co-operation may be the name of the game in the near
future. The Japanese greatly admire new ideas—
which I believe we have. Of course, these are early
days and this trip is purely a fact-finding one.
Co-operation may be a long way away and demand
more in the way of understanding and loyalty—'his
dark eyes moved slowly from Philippa to Sam to Rex
and back again '—than is possible. But in the end we
may find the trip has been well worth while and at the
very least we can make some new contacts and renew
old ones.'

There was a polite murmur of assent from Sam
and Rex, and Matthew Vane sat down, crossing his

long legs casually. 'Now, to details. I understand that you've been informed of flight time and that you already have your tickets, so the best thing is for you all to make your own way and meet up on the plane. It's a long and tedious journey, as I'm sure you know, so bring plenty of reading matter. If it's work-orientated reading matter so much the better.' He smiled, an on-off smile that didn't reach his dark, searching eyes. The Great Man unbending and being chummy with the peasants! Philippa thought cynically. Oh yes, she knew the type.

'One other thing,' he continued smoothly, 'there's been a change on the personnel side. Adrian Banks, who was to have led the team, has been transferred to another assignment, so you won't, therefore, have the pleasure of his company.'

From a long distance away Philippa heard murmurs of surprise from Sam and Rex. Her eyes were fixed on Matthew Vane and he was looking straight back at her, his hard face expressionless. She felt a jolt of disappointment. She had looked forward to the trip, but not least she had looked forward to being with Adrian, getting to know him better, finding more things to share. And now—this!

Her mouth was dry and she took a gulp of her sherry, swallowed it awkwardly, and was assailed by an embarrassing cough. The dark glance of Matthew Vane was still fixed on her as he added, 'I have to warn you that in place of Banks you're going to have to put up with me.'

Polite murmurs again from Sam and Rex. Philippa said nothing. She hardly listened as the deep, slightly drawling voice went on adding a few encouraging pleasantries about the trip. 'Head Office is setting quite a store by it—efforts won't go unrecognised—plenty of time for detailed plans when we arrive——' He stood up. 'Any questions?'

There were questions, but of course she couldn't ask them. Why had Adrian been taken off the assignment at the last moment? What had happened? Had it been judged that he wasn't capable of doing the job? Had he slipped up over something and come into conflict with the directors at Head Office? Had he had a row with Matthew Vane and had that dictatorial individual demoted him just out of spite?

That last seemed to Philippa the most likely explanation, and suddenly she had a strong urge to opt out. To say she had changed her mind, she didn't want to go on this trip after all. She would have loved to see Matthew Vane's face if she did that. He must be thinking that it was a wonderful opportunity for her—a junior member of the department—to be included in the team. Which, in all honesty, she had to admit it was.

And of course she couldn't refuse to go; that would be as good as saying that she was more interested in Adrian Banks than in doing her job, and that wasn't true. She was *very* interested in her job and she knew she was lucky to have it. But as she followed Sam and Rex down the narrow, softly carpeted staircase most of the spring had gone out of her step.

By now it was after six o'clock and everyone had left. It was a dark evening and drizzling rain obscured the big windows on the first-floor landing. Rex pulled out a packet and stuck a limp, unlighted cigarette between his lips. Smoking was forbidden inside the building and the rule was strictly enforced.

Sam stopped on the landing and whistled expressively. 'Well, that's a turn-up for the books! The boss himself coming along with us instead of Banks. No skin off my nose,' he added. He glanced towards Philippa and seemed about to say something else, but then stopped.

Instead he turned to Rex. 'You've got all the gen on Series KB, haven't you?'

Rex nodded. 'Took it home with me last night to tidy up the loose ends.'

Sam gave him a quick hard look. 'Well, don't forget to bring it along with you tomorrow. I don't know if we'll need it, but we might.'

'Will do,' said Rex, making for the head of the stairs with his quick, shambling, head-bent-forward walk. 'I'll be off, then. See you both tomorrow.'

When he had disappeared round the turn of the stairs Sam grinned at Philippa. 'Can't get out quick enough to light his fag, the poor so-and-so! I suppose you can understand it. I'd probably smoke myself into an early grave if I had old Rex's problems.' He frowned. 'He's not been too on the ball lately in his work. Taking all that KB stuff home with him isn't really on, but I can't very well bawl him out about it.'

Philippa nodded. Rex Hanling didn't confide much in other members of the staff, but it was known that he was separated from his wife and lived alone in digs in Stratford-on-Avon and that his elderly mother was in a nursing home somewhere. Philippa had heard from Mona Drew, in the downstairs office, that Rex had been in charge of software research until Sam had been brought in. 'Over poor old Rex's head,' Mona had confided.

There was nothing that went on in the office that Mona didn't know about. 'Rex must have felt pretty sick at the time, but he's not the sort to make a fuss or walk out in a pet. So I guess he decided to grin and bear it.'

Philippa was sorry for Rex, although she tried not to let him see it. He was 'poor old Rex', one of the world's losers, good enough at his job but totally eclipsed by Sam Gunner, who seemed to manipulate his computer as a concert pianist would play his piano, with a kind of brilliant, intuitive genius that left Rex far behind. Rex had been looking rotten lately, she thought, pale and anxious. Perhaps the Tokyo trip would cheer him up. She certainly hoped so.

'How about getting to the airport tomorrow?' Sam was saying to her. He looked faintly embarrassed. 'I didn't mention it to you before because I guessed you might have fixed up something with Adrian, but as it seems he won't be going——' He glanced at Philippa's face and went on quickly, 'I'll be catching the early train from Leamington to Reading myself. If you decide to go that way I'll look out for you.'

Philippa gave him a bright smile. 'Thanks, Sam, I might do that. But don't wait for me—I'm not quite sure of plans yet. Anyway, see you on the plane.'

She said good night and went off along the corridor to the girls' rest-room. Here she sank dispiritedly into a chair. It was silly, she told herself, to be *so* disappointed. After all, Adrian was only a friend, it wasn't as if she were in love with him.

But you were half inclined to fall in love with him, weren't you? You were ready for fun, for the excitement of feeling young and alive again, she told herself.

There hadn't been much fun since the break-up with Gerald. And before she had got over that her grandmother had been taken ill. Life had narrowed down to the daytime stress of keeping up with the job, and the evenings when she hurried home to do late-night shopping, to cook meals, to sit with Gran, who had seen nobody all day but the district nurse. Later the visits to the hospital each evening had replaced some of the chores at home, but Gran's terminal illness cast a deep shadow over everything, however much they both tried to keep cheerful.

But now it was over, the willing bondage. Now she was free. Alone, but free, and the immediate future had beckoned excitingly. Tokyo with Adrian—a double plus. Tokyo with the arrogant, formidable Matthew Vane could be counted a large minus as well as a plus. She hoped they wouldn't cancel each other out.

She tried to look on the bright side. She probably wouldn't need to see very much of the man in Tokyo; she would be Sam's assistant, as she was here. And Adrian would still be here when she got back; they could take up their friendship where they left off. An idea occurred to her: she would call in at his hotel on her way home, just to commiserate with him and say goodbye. Cheered by the prospect of seeing him again, she got up and swilled her face and renewed her make-up before she took her short jacket from her locker and swung it round her shoulders as she went out into the empty corridor.

Everyone had left by now, and as she crossed the wide landing, her heels tapping on the polished wood floor, a sound from behind made her look round. Matthew Vane was closing the door at the bottom of his private staircase and coming towards her. She acknowledged his presence by the faintest of nods— surely protocol didn't demand that she stand aside and allow him to go down the main staircase ahead of her?—and walked on.

'Miss Marsden.' The deep, drawling voice halted her, but she wasn't going to turn back and walk towards him—why should she? She stood where she was, at the top of the stairs, straight and slim, her coppery hair framing her small, composed face, and waited until he came up beside her.

He stopped and studied her face in silence for what seemed ages, and was probably a matter of seconds. She squirmed inside. Why did he have to keep looking at her like that, as if she were up for sale and he was assessing her value?

'Yes, Mr Vane?' she queried in a cool little voice.

'About tomorrow.' He placed one long-fingered hand on the carved post at the top of the stairway. He was standing close to her, too close for comfort, because there was something about the sheer size of the man, the unseen but undoubted hardness of the body beneath the well-fitting clothes, that made her feel breathless. She would have liked to move away, but her feet appeared to be rooted to the polished wood of the floor.

'Yes?' she said again.

'I propose to drive to the airport—I'll pick you up and take you along with me. If you'll give me your address it will save me looking it up in the files—the downstairs office will be closed by now.'

Philippa drew in a breath. 'Thank you, Mr Vane,

but I've already made my own arrangements.'

He frowned. 'What arrangements?' he rapped out.

Bully! High-handed bully. She lifted her chin a fraction. 'I've arranged to travel by train to Reading,' she improvised quickly, thinking of Sam and his rather shy invitation to meet her.

Matthew Vane's mouth curved ironically. 'That was a spur-of-the-moment decision, wasn't it? I'm willing to bet you were depending on Banks to get you to the airport. And as I'm taking over his role I may as well start off on the right foot.'

The cheek of the man! Philippa's fist clenched. She'd like to hit out at him, to wipe that nasty sneer off his mouth.

'You'll be picking up Sam and Rex too, I take it?' she said distantly.

'Oh no, certainly not.' The ironic smile appeared again. 'Surely you've been with the firm long enough, Miss Marsden, to understand that there is a certain hierarchy in these matters, however we may deplore it. Sam and Rex will make their own way.'

'But I'm the junior in the department,' she began.

'In the office—yes,' he agreed. 'But on the Japanese trip you will be working closely with me—as my personal assistant. That makes a difference.'

'Your personal assistant?' she echoed. 'I'm not—I mean, I'm not on the secretarial staff, I'm a qualified computer programmer.'

'Quite,' he said crisply. 'You're also, naturally, an expert with a word processor, which means you have no difficulty handling any sort of keyboard. You've taken a course in audio-typing, which may be useful. And you——'

Philippa was really angry now. 'I assume that you've been going through my personal files, Mr Vane?' Her cheeks were flushed, her eyes flashed blue fire.

'Of course,' he said. 'I wouldn't choose a personal assistant without vetting that person's credentials very thoroughly.'

'There's just one thing you've forgotten, though.'

'And that is?'

'You've forgotten to enquire whether I'm willing to take on the job.'

'Ah!' He breathed the word and then was silent. His dark eyes, looking thoughtfully into hers, began to have a very strange effect on her. She found herself quite unable to look away; she was being magnetised—hypnotised—held in subjection under the impact of that direct, unsmiling gaze.

'Very remiss of me,' Matthew Vane drawled at last. Then, quite suddenly, he smiled, a real smile that took her by surprise. Almost against her will she felt her own lips parting into an answering smile, which she quickly suppressed.

'I'm asking you now,' he said.

Philippa swallowed and opened her mouth to speak, but nothing came. She was conscious only of the strong face above her own; of the near-black eyes with their long, curving lashes, eyes that scrutinised her narrowly but told her nothing of what was going on in the brain behind them. Of the whiteness of the smile that showed in a thin line between his slightly-parted lips. Gerald used to smile at her like that when he wanted something from her. 'Well?' Matthew Vane said quite gently.

Her throat was dry.

'I—all right,' she muttered.

'Good,' he said briskly, and she knew that he had never for one moment doubted her reply.

The smile disappeared. He took a notebook from an inside pocket and looked down at her enquiringly, pencil poised.

'Now,' he said. 'The address, please.'

CHAPTER TWO

THE rain was pouring down when the bus deposited Philippa in Warwick half an hour later. She had had a long wait for a bus and was unpleasantly wet. Her sandals felt soggy and there was an icy patch between her shoulders where her jacket was beginning to let the rain through. Silly of her not to bring an umbrella this morning, but she had counted on getting a lift from Adrian.

She hesitated for a moment about going into the Lord Leycester Hotel looking like an orphan of the storm, but the need to see Adrian and find out, if she could, what had happened outweighed any qualms she might have about her appearance.

The entrance hall appeared to be empty. Philippa stood looking round for the receptionist, shivering slightly. Perhaps she had caught a chill—perhaps she would be really ill by tomorrow and not fit to fly. She couldn't decide whether she would be glad or sorry.

A movement on her right made her turn to see Adrian coming down the stairs.

'Philippa!' He came towards her and she thought he hesitated slightly before he smiled and asked, 'Where did you spring from?'

It was hardly a glad welcome, but he was probably not feeling too pleased with life just now. To have one's plans changed at the last moment must be extremely frustrating.

'From the bus,' she said. 'I found myself right outside the hotel and thought I'd look in and see if you were here and say how sorry I am you won't be coming with us tomorrow.' That sounded just right, she considered: sufficiently disappointed without being dramatic, or making too much of their friendship.

'You've heard, then?'

She nodded. 'We've just had a briefing with Matthew Vane.'

Adrian's fair eyebrows went up. 'A session with God Almighty—how nice for you!'

Philippa met his eyes with a grin and the tacit agreement between them seemed to have a relaxing effect on Adrian. He put a hand on the shoulder of her light jacket. 'My dear girl, you're soaking wet!' He seemed to hesitate again for a moment, then he said, 'Look, come up to my room and we'll dry you off. It's on the first floor, we won't wait for the lift.' He led her towards the staircase, his arm still round her shoulder.

His room was obviously one of the best rooms in the hotel, large and comfortably furnished. It must cost the earth to live here; no wonder he was going to look for a flat!

He came up behind her, drew off her wet jacket, and draped it over a chair beside the radiator. Then he poured out a drink and handed it to her. 'Sit down and drink this, it'll warm you up.'

Philippa sipped the brandy. 'This is kind of you, Adrian. I didn't intend to park myself on you like this.'

He waved that away. 'My dear girl, I'm delighted.' The hesitation that she had noticed at first had disappeared now. He seemed genuinely pleased she was there.

He took a long swig of his drink and leaned back in his chair. 'Now tell me, what story did Matt Vane spin to account for the fact that he was going to take my place in the Tokyo team?' His lip curled. It was obvious that he didn't like the high-handed Mr Vane any more than she did.

'He just said that Head Office had put you on another assignment,' she told him.

'H'm.' He nodded slowly. 'A good story, but I don't imagine Head Office had anything to do with it.'

Philippa frowned puzzledly. 'Then why—I don't understand. If he'd wanted to go himself he could have arranged it that way earlier. Why did he have to change things at the last moment?'

Adrian looked thoughtfully into his glass. Then he smiled and shrugged. 'Oh, I don't know—probably he just fancied the trip. Have a drop more?' He leaned forward to take her glass.

She covered it with her hand. 'No, thanks, I've had enough. Adrian, there *is* something you're not telling me, isn't there? I've got to work as Matthew Vane's personal assistant on this trip—he's just told me that. If there's anything about him that I ought to know, please tell me.'

Again he hesitated. Then he seemed to make up his mind. 'Between the two of us——' he began. 'No, I don't think I should say this.'

She waited and after another moment or two he went on more steadily, 'I'm not usually mistaken about people—it's my job—so I know I can trust you, Philippa, when I ask you to keep it under your hat. It may be only my nasty suspicious nature—' he gave her a wry smile '—but I've thought for a few weeks that something funny's going on in the department. As you know, a lot of the work is hush-hush.'

Philippa nodded. 'Especially in our office.'

'Exactly. Well, doesn't it strike you as a bit strange that you three in the office have to put all sorts of safeguards on, and yet, when you've gone home, Matthew Vane has the whole place to himself, to come and go in and out of the offices as he pleases?'

'But——' Philippa began. 'He wouldn't——'

'Hear me out.' Adrian put a hand on her knee. It felt warm through her thin, damp skirt. 'I told you it was only a suspicion, but—well, I know a chap at Head Office—we get together for drinks occasionally—and he was telling me in confidence that there's a bit of a scare on about industrial espionage. Some of our new software seems to be finding its way into our competitors' hands. As you know, I'm a ninny about high-tech, I don't really know the first thing about a computer program. But Matthew Vane does. He's an expert. Before he took this job he was head research man with Morgan Triffin Electronics. Did you know that?'

'In New York?'

'Precisely. And it's in New York that some of our new ideas have been turning up. Not at Morgan Triffin's—at another, smaller company.'

There was a silence while Philippa tried to digest what Adrian was hinting at. At last she said, 'You mean you think Matthew Vane may be passing on confidential information to someone outside the company?'

Adrian laughed rather uneasily. 'Oh, my dear, don't quote me on that! I just wondered, that's all. I happened to look in at my office one evening last week—some work I meant to do at home and I needed the info. As I was coming up the stairs I saw Vane coming out of your office and locking the door behind him.'

Philippa's eyes widened. 'Wh-what happened?'

He laughed again. 'Oh, nothing happened. No cloak and dagger stuff. We just sort of—looked at each other and I said, "Hullo—something I forgot," or words to that effect, and went into my office to get the papers. Of course, the head of the branch didn't have to explain to me why he was creeping round the office when everyone had left. He just nodded and stared at me in that withering way of his and went up to his flat.'

Philippa was silent again, her eyes searching Adrian's fair, open face. Then she said slowly, 'Adrian, after what you've just said, I don't think I could possibly go on this trip to Tokyo. I couldn't work with the man knowing—wondering—I mean——'

'But you must, my dear, you simply must.' Adrian leaned forward eagerly. 'Don't you see, it's a matter of loyalty to the company. You'll have a priceless opportunity, as his personal assistant, to keep your eyes and ears open. You're a bright girl, if he's got some funny business going you might spot it.'

'Oh yes, and then what do I do? Confront him with the evidence?' Philippa's laugh was unsteady. She might joke about it, but the very idea of challenging Matthew Vane, of looking into that hard, ruthless face and accusing him of dishonesty, made her stomach feel queasy.

Adrian was laughing too. 'Oh, my sweet child,

you're too straightforward—you need to be more subtle about these things.'

'You mean, you want me to spy on him?'

'No, no, *no*!' He threw up his hands in comical despair. 'You've got the wrong idea. I'm not asking you to do anything more than keep a watchful eye open while you're with him in Tokyo. If he *is* on the fiddle he may have contacts in Japan, and that may be why he's decided to go there at the last moment.'

'And if I find out anything? Always assuming that I do go,' she added.

'Well——' He spread out his hands. 'I suppose the best thing is to contact me when you get back, and we can talk it over and decide if there's any action that should be taken.'

Philippa bit her lip hard. This was the second shock she had had this evening and it was even more disastrous than the first. It was against everything in her nature to snoop, to prevaricate. 'I'd much rather not go at all,' she said slowly. 'Do you really think I should?'

He took both her hands in his. 'I really think you should, Pippa dear,' he said firmly. 'You owe it to the company. The fellow might be losing them millions—and picking up a packet for himself at the same time.'

Adrian really was worried. It must be a difficult position for him, to suspect a fellow worker—and the top man in the branch at that. He could so easily turn his back and forget the whole thing. But it was clear that he had the good of the company at heart. She thought that she'd never met a man she admired or respected more. She wanted to please him, to make him think of her as a girl who could rise to a challenge. He wouldn't be interested in a poor, weak, timid female.

'O.K.,' she said suddenly, 'I'll go.' And was rewarded by his warm smile of approval.

'Good girl, I knew I wasn't mistaken in you, Pippa.' He got to his feet. 'And now, much as I hate to turn you out, I'm afraid I must. I've got a train to catch. This new assignment that someone—*someone*—' he stressed the word darkly '—has thought up for me out of the blue.'

Philippa jumped up immediately. 'Oh, goodness, why didn't you tell me?' She snatched her jacket from the back of the chair; it was still damp and she hung it over her arm rather than put it on.

Adrian glanced at his watch. 'I've got a taxi ordered to take me to the station in Leamington. I could drop you off at the end of your road.'

They went to the door together, and Adrian paused, putting a hand on her shoulder. 'I'm really horribly disappointed about Tokyo,' he said softly, 'I was looking forward no end to sharing the trip with you. We could have had such fun together, Pippa. We get on well, don't we?'

She nodded speechlessly, all the disappointment welling back.

His face was close to hers. 'You're so lovely,' he whispered. He bent his head and kissed her, a friendly, undemanding kiss. Then the telephone rang on the bedside table, and he went across to answer it.

'Yes?' he said, lifting the receiver impatiently. 'Right, thanks.'

He came back to Philippa. 'The taxi's here.' He put his arms round her and kissed again, and this time the kiss lasted longer and she felt him tremble against her. 'Hell,' he muttered, 'why do I have to catch that train?'

He drew in a breath. 'Luck's against me all the way today,' he said very wryly. 'Come on, Pippa, let's go down while I'm still capable of saying goodbye to you.' He picked up the travel-bag beside the door and, with his other arm round her waist, they walked down the stairs together.

They had almost reached the bottom when Philippa felt the pressure of his arm tighten. 'Look who's here,' he muttered into her ear.

She looked across the foyer to see Matthew Vane coming in through the front entrance door, and she felt her inside tighten with something that felt like fear. He had changed into a dark grey suit, with a white shirt and a silky, burgundy tie and his black hair gleamed under the lighting in the foyer. By his side was a girl—tall and blonde and slim and very exquisite. She wore a black suit with a tight, slit skirt and lots of jewellery, and a short jacket of silky white fun-fur was slung with careless elegance round her shoulders. One hand rested possessively on her companion's sleeve and she was laughing up at him.

There was no way the couples could avoid each other. The two who had just come in were heading for the reception desk and Adrian had his room key in the hand that was round Philippa's waist. He took his hand away and passed the key to the girl at the desk. 'Back on Friday, Nora,' he said to the receptionist.

She smiled at him. 'Right, Mr Banks. Have a good trip.'

Matthew Vane and the girl had reached the desk

now. His dark glance went from Adrian to Philippa, standing a little to one side, and back again. 'Just leaving?' he said amiably, as one colleague to another.

'That's right.' Philippa could sense the tension between the two men as Adrian gave the newcomers a cool stare.

The blonde girl's expertly made-up eyes passed over Philippa, standing there in her office blouse and skirt, her hair lank with the rain, her light jacket hanging limply over her arm, and rested on Adrian with the kind of interest that she would probably show in any new man.

Adrian replaced his arm round Philippa's waist. 'Sorry we must rush, we've got a taxi waiting. Come along, Pippa.' He urged Philippa towards the door and she went with him, but not before she had caught a whiff of some exclusive perfume as she passed the girl, and had seen the dark, amused glance of Matthew Vane fixed on her. Damn the man, why did he have to be so disgustingly superior?

'Expensive tastes he's got,' Adrian said sourly as they got into the taxi. 'Did you see who that was?'

'The girl?' Philippa shook her head. 'No.'

'Heidi Jones. She's the Chairman's secretary, if you can call it that. I've heard that Vane's been going round with her—getting her up here for weekends. I'd have thought he'd go to Birmingham, there aren't many bright lights in Warwick. But perhaps they make their own amusements up in his penthouse.'

Philippa had a quick vision of Matthew Vane and the beautiful Heidi Jones climbing the narrow carpeted staircase to his flat, laughing together, closing the oak door behind them, melting into each other's arms in the darkness——

'Will this do you?' The taxi had stopped at the end of the road where Philippa was staying. She blinked, looking out. 'Yes, this will be fine, thanks.'

Adrian got out and opened the door for her. 'Goodbye, Pippa dear,' he said warmly. 'Don't forget, will you?'

'I won't,' she promised, and added impulsively, 'Oh, I wish you were coming tomorrow, Adrian.'

'Me too,' he said, and kissed her quickly before he got back into the taxi. It rattled away along the main road and she stood for a moment, watching it go.

The rain had almost stopped and she walked slowly along the lamplit road towards the small terraced house where she was living with Gran's friends, the Smithsons. All the pleasure and anticipation had gone out of the Tokyo trip now. She would have enjoyed every minute if Adrian had been there, but instead she would have to put up with that hateful Matthew Vane, with his dictatorial, high-handed ways. He was the kind of man she most disliked and it would be a real ordeal to work with him, even for the inside of a week. For some reason seeing him with that gorgeous girl had made her dislike him even more. She would get away as much as possible in what spare time she had, and be with Sam and Rex. She would be comfortable in their company.

As for Adrian's suspicions—well, she didn't intend to play the lady detective. It was difficult to see what she could find out, but if she noticed anything that seemed strange she would make a note of it and perhaps mention it to Adrian when she got back. That was as far as she was prepared to go.

She sighed as she turned her key in the front door of the Smithsons' terrace house, thinking of what she still had to do. She must wash her hair, but she hadn't the heart, now, to try out the new conditioner. She had no wish to put lights in her hair for Mr Matthew Vane.

'Well, dear, is there anything I can help you with? Any ironing or anything? Tom's out at his club this evening and my time's my own.'

Mrs Smithson collected the supper dishes and bore them off to the kitchen as she spoke. She was a little birdlike woman with a surplus of energy for a seventy-year-old and a lively interest in what was going on around her. Philippa's trip to Tokyo had been the main topic of conversation in the Smithson household for the past fortnight.

Philippa folded her napkin and stood up. 'I think I'm in control, thanks all the same, Mrs Smithson. I'll wash my hair now—so long as it won't use too much hot water.'

'Don't you worry about that, dear. You use as much as you like. I won't wash up tonight, I'll put the dishes in to soak and do them all in the morning when you've gone.' She dumped the pile of dishes in the sink. 'What time will this man be calling for you? Oh dear, isn't it a pity that nice Mr Banks won't be going?' Adrian had come in for a few minutes on one occasion when he had brought Philippa home and Mrs Smithson had been enthusing about him ever since. 'It would have been lovely if he had been going to Japan with you, wouldn't it? But perhaps this other man will be nice—what did you say his name is?'

Nice, thought Philippa wryly, as she supplied the information. Nobody in their right mind would call Matthew Vane *nice*. As she went upstairs she wondered what adjective you could apply to him and came up with the one that Adrian had used. *Withering*. Yes, that was what he was. He looked at you and made you feel conscious of yourself. He played havoc with your confidence.

That was probably his way of running the branch and the staff in it. But not me, she vowed. She wasn't going to be crushed under any jackboot. She pushed the rubber spray-gadget on to the taps in the bathroom with a vicious shove. 'Not me,' she muttered aloud, rubbing the lather into her hair energetically, as if she were already showing Mr Matthew Vane that she was made of stronger stuff. At that point she managed to get lather into her eyes and cursed aloud. That was *his* fault too.

She finished the rinsing in a more decorous manner. Stupid to let a man she hardly knew get under her skin like this. All she had to do was carry out the work he gave her to the best of her ability, and she had plenty of confidence in that. She knew her job, and she had picked up a good deal of the work that Sam and Rex were doing since she had been at the Manor. Very soon, she felt, they would include her in some of their more advanced programming, and she was looking forward to the challenge of that.

In view of that, she decided, as she brush-dried her coppery hair into its usual style, curving softly into her neck, she really didn't have to allow Mr Matthew Vane to practise his dismissive, overbearing tactics on her.

When her hair was dry she finished packing while Mrs Smithson hovered in the doorway, hoping to be asked to help, and chatting away until Philippa could have yelled with sheer nerves.

Packing was tricky. 'Travel light—put everything in a bag you can take inside the plane with you,' Adrian had told her, and she was determined to forget nothing, to have everything ready if That Man was calling for her in the morning. She wouldn't keep him waiting a second. She wouldn't give him any chance to fault her.

Two light dresses—undies, tights, nighties. Toilet things to go in at the last minute tomorrow morning. Passport, traveller's cheques, airline ticket in her handbag.

'Will it be hot in Japan?' Mrs Smithson's voice broke into her concentration. 'You'll want a light coat, won't you, in case the evenings turn cold. Will the cherry blossom be out in April? There was a lovely programme on last week, all about the Japanese. Those huge men with terrifying swords—sam—sam something.'

'Samurai,' said Philippa absently. She had been immersing herself in literature about Japan and its history for the last fortnight. 'I don't think there are many of them about now.' Handkerchiefs, she thought, pulling out a top drawer. Oh, and emery boards. An extra pair of light sandals, perhaps. She stuffed them down the side of the bag.

'Would you like a cup of tea, dear?' Mrs Smithson's voice sounded a bit pathetic and Philippa turned quickly. 'Oh yes, please, that would be lovely.' Dear Mrs S., she meant well, though she could be rather trying. And she was going to feel flat after all the excitement was over. 'Yes, let's have a nice cup of tea.'

Philippa slept uneasily that night and wakened to a bad attack of jitters, such as she hadn't had since the day of her finals at college. She couldn't eat much breakfast in spite of Mrs Smithson's anxious fussing, and as soon as it was over she went up to her room to wait. She checked her handbag once again, zipped up the holdall which she would take inside the plane with her, and went to the mirror to reassure herself about her appearance.

To travel in she had chosen to wear an uncrushable acrylic suit in pearl-grey with a navy crêpe-de-chine blouse. Navy tights and sandals with slim ankle straps, a navy kid bag. She would carry her shower-coat over her arm. Her coppery hair looked clean and glossy, her light make-up was faultless.

She twisted round, examining the effect from every angle. Picture of a confident young career woman, setting out on her first important trip abroad. Yes, she would do; she would even be able to meet Matthew Vane's sardonic scrutiny with confidence. She just wished she didn't have this faint churning inside.

A car sounded in the quiet street and pulled up outside the house. The front door bell rang and Mrs Smithson's step pattered across the tiled hall. Voices. Mrs Smithson's fluttering laugh. A man's deep voice replying. Already Philippa felt that she would recognise that voice anywhere. It was peculiar how it seemed to echo deep inside her.

The bedroom door opened and Mrs Smithson's face appeared round it, the cheeks pink, the eyes wide. 'He's here,' she mouthed. 'In a *Rolls*, my dear, and with a *chauffeur!* And he's so *handsome!*'

'The chauffeur?' teased Philippa. She picked up her handbag and holdall from the bed. Now that the moment had arrived she felt suddenly quite calm. How silly she'd been, there was nothing to be nervous about. She smiled at Mrs Smithson and marched down the stairs.

It was a beautiful fresh April morning after the rain last night. The sun glinted on the dark green satin bonnet of the Rolls. The uniformed chauffeur put Philippa's bag in the boot. Matthew Vane was standing by the door of the car, and Philippa didn't have to look twice to see why Mrs Smithson had been so impressed. Everything about the man was impressive—his height, his dark good looks, his well-cut charcoal grey suit, his air of casual confidence.

'Hullo, Miss Marsden. All set?' Pleasant, businesslike.

'Good morning, Mr Vane. Yes, I'm quite ready.' She turned and kissed Mrs Smithson, who was fluttering and pink-cheeked as Matthew Vane nodded to her courteously. He opened the back door of the car and Philippa climbed in and sank back into the soft leather seat. The chauffeur slammed the door of the boot and got behind the steering-wheel, and, to Philippa's relief, Matthew Vane took the passenger seat in the front.

He turned round to her and said, 'I'm glad to see you've brought only hand-baggage; that was sensible.'

Well, at least that was a good start. As the big car slid away from the kerb she turned round and waved to Mrs Smithson through the back window. It was quite absurd, she was only going away for a short business trip, but she had the feeling that a part of her life was over.

The bustling activity of the huge, crowded terminal at Heathrow was new to Philippa, and she admitted frankly to herself that it was comforting to have a large and experienced male beside her to take effortless charge of everything—luggage, passports, tickets—and get her safely on to the plane.

As they were welcomed into the cabin by a smiling stewardess Philippa looked around her with surprise. She had flown abroad only once before—to Belgium with a school party. That flight had started from Birmingham, and certainly the accommodation had been nothing like this—roomy and luxurious. On that trip it had more resembled the packing of sardines into a tin.

'Window seat?' enquired Matthew Vane politely. She sank into a seat and he took the one beside her. She seemed to remember, before, that there had been three or more seats abreast. The seats in this cabin were much wider and more comfortable.

Philippa looked around. 'Where are Sam and Rex? Shouldn't we be contacting them?'

'Later,' he said. 'Have you forgotten that hierarchy that I spoke about yesterday?' His dark glance quizzed her. 'They'll be quite happy further back.'

Philippa looked around, frowning, and then the explanation dawned on her. 'We're travelling first-class, aren't we?'

'Correct,' he said.

'And Sam and Rex are in the tourist class?'

'Right again.' He looked amused. He might have

been encouraging a bright child. 'Any objections?'

'Yes, I think I have,' she said stiffly. 'I don't feel like one of the privileged few and I'm not sure I like it. It makes me uncomfortable.'

She didn't care for the way he smiled. 'Then you'd better take the matter up with your friend Adrian Banks when you get back,' he said smoothly. 'He was responsible for all the bookings. Incidentally, he'd have had something to account for when he turned in his expenses. Only board directors are allowed first-class travel on long-haul flights, and he certainly isn't a board director.'

'And you are?' Philippa enquired with a limpid glance.

He nodded briefly. 'I suppose you can't blame the chap—doubtless he wanted to get you to himself on the trip. Very romantic!' His lip curled faintly.

The cabin was filling up, mostly with well-heeled businessmen, but there were also one or two expensively dressed and coiffured women.

'I don't know what you mean,' Philippa said shortly, lowering her voice. 'There isn't anything like—like that between Adrian and myself.'

'Just good friends?' Matthew Vane mocked.

'Yes,' she snapped, remembering too late how he must have seen Adrian and herself coming down from his bedroom at the hotel last night; how Adrian had been holding her close against him; how her jacket had been slung over her arm as if she had been interrupted in the middle of dressing. She felt the heat rising into her cheeks. Oh well, let the wretched man think the worst if he wanted to, she didn't care what he thought of her. She turned away from him and stared unseeingly out of the window.

Matthew Vane reached over and covered her hand with his. 'Relax,' he said. 'We've got a long way to go. If you keep this up you'll be exhausted before we take off.'

She looked down at the hand resting on hers. His touch was warm and light, and it disturbed her because it was so unexpected. 'Keep what up?' she muttered.

'Antagonism,' he said. 'Takes a lot out of you. Makes you tense.'

She *was* tense. She felt rigid, every muscle stretched tight. She wished he would take his hand from hers.

'I'm not antagonistic. Why should I be?'

'Why, indeed?' His eyes moved lazily over her face. 'I'm a very friendly animal. I don't bite—not often, anyway.' A smile crinkled the skin beside his eyes. 'I see your difficulty, of course,' he added suavely. 'You were expecting Adrian Banks to be with you on this trip and were looking forward, no doubt, to having an enjoyable time with such a beautiful young man.'

'Yes, I was,' she returned, lifting her chin a fraction, 'although I don't care for your choice of adjectives.'

'I could think of some other ones,' he said, and he removed his hand from hers, 'but you would probably like them less.'

The cabin staff had begun their routine instructions about safety regulations, and Philippa darted a glance at the face of the man beside her. The amused, ironic look had disappeared and his mouth had drawn into a tight line. He really disliked Adrian, didn't he? Could it be true, what Adrian had said, that this man was defrauding the company and knew that Adrian suspected him? She thrust the suspicion away. She had to work with Matthew Vane on this trip and if she began to see dark significances in every look, every word, life would be intolerable.

Seat-belts were fastened. Soon the big jumbo taxied, turned, taxied again and was airborne. Philippa looked down at the airport buildings getting smaller and smaller, at the sprawl of London below, buildings first densely cluttered, then thinning out, and finally merging, in turn, into the green of the Home Counties. They were on their way, and she couldn't help feeling a little lift in her spirits.

On the intercom the captain's voice informed them that the flying weather was excellent, gave details of the route, of the height, wished them a pleasant journey. A smiling stewardess served champagne, another took orders for lunch. Philippa lay back in her extremely comfortable seat and sipped the champagne and thought, This is luxury travel. What are you worrying about? You're off on a trip that thousands of girls would envy. Certainly you're disappointed that Adrian isn't here, but not heartbroken, and you'd be stupid to let Matthew Vane spoil everything for you.

Almost as if he could guess her thoughts he turned towards her and smiled. 'O.K., Philippa? Not nervous of flying?'

She was startled by the way her inside gave a jolt as he spoke her name for the first time in that deep voice of his. And suddenly she was aware of herself sitting there in her pearl-grey suit that had cost her nearly a week's wages, her hair curving into her neck, her make-up faultless, and beside her the best-looking man she had ever met. She was aware of his strong man's body, close to hers, of the long legs and powerfully muscled thighs, of the slim brown fingers holding his glass. All the corny things you are supposed to notice in a man who—who attracts you immediately. But of course he didn't attract her. What she felt was simply the working of the old male-female thing. Physical, nothing more, and as old as humanity itself. And Matthew Vane was a very physically impressive man. She might as well admit that at the beginning.

'Not a bit nervous, thanks,' she said coolly, but not quite truthfully.

He nodded. 'Good. Here's to a pleasant journey, then.' He lifted his champagne glass.

'A pleasant journey,' echoed Philippa.

He opened his briefcase and took out a wad of papers. 'You'll forgive me if I devote most of the time to work?'

'Of course.' She almost laughed. He didn't think she expected him to indulge in light conversation, did he? She took a paperback from her holdall.

Matthew Vane glanced at the title. '*A Wreath for the Bridegroom*—are you a mystery addict, Philippa?' She caught the ironic tone again. What did he expect her to read on a long journey, for goodness' sake? *The Fall of the Roman Empire*?

'Not an addict,' she said rather shortly. 'I enjoy a well-written detective story.' What would you say, Mr Matthew Vane, if you knew I had my eye on you?

'And do you always find out whodunnit before the sleuth does?'

'Sometimes I do.' She met his amused glance

coolly. 'Sometimes not. When I do it's mostly guesswork,' she admitted.

'Woman's famous intuition?' he mocked.

She refused to be needled. 'You could say that.'

'And what else do you read? Love stories?

'Those too, when I'm in the mood.'

'Ah,' he smiled—patronisingly, she thought. 'I must remember that,' and turned back to his papers.

Fifteen hours' flying had seemed a long time to Philippa and she was quite surprised to find how quickly the hours were passing. She determined to make the most of this luxury interlude in her life, and not let it be spoiled by regrets about Adrian's absence or irritation about her treatment at the hands of the formidable Matthew Vane.

She was glad when dinner was served. She had been much too excited to eat much lunch and the very sight of the large bill of fare with a photograph of the Tokyo Imperial Palace on the cover made her mouth water.

Matthew Vane was consulting with the waitress. Then he turned to Philippa. 'What's your fancy?'

'It all sounds wonderful,' she said. 'I admit to feeling very hungry and extremely greedy!'

He chuckled, and that was a sound she hadn't heard from his lips before. 'That lets me out, then. I admit to a similar weakness. And good cooking is one of the perks of travelling first class. I'm glad your principles will allow you to enjoy it.' The smile he slid towards her was definitely teasing and Philippa felt her resistance beginning to crumble slightly. Perhaps he could be fun, after all.

She consulted the menu. 'Japanese Delicacies?' she read aloud. 'Konjak String Beef Roll, Baby

Abalone, Ginko Nuts.' She wrinkled her nose. 'I'm not sure about the Baby Abalone—it has a sinister sound.'

'It might be safer to stick to the poached salmon,' Matthew advised solemnly. 'I'll introduce you to Japanese food when we get there.'

'You know Japan well?' asked Philippa, when their orders had been given.

'You can never claim that you know Japan well unless you're Japanese. But I've been there several times. I find Tokyo a fascinating and exciting city.'

'Oh, I'm sure it is. I can't wait to get there.' Philippa's blue eyes danced. 'Tell me about it.' She forgot about disappointment, antagonism. As they ate their way through the poached salmon, roast rack of lamb with almond croquette potatoes and green peas with tiny pearl onions, she listened, absorbed, while Matthew talked about Japan and its history. He talked well and she would have found it entertaining even if she hadn't been interested in Japan. By the time they had passed through the cheese, fruit, and gâteau stages and arrived at the Irish coffee with pralines, consuming a bottle of red wine of Matthew's choosing on the way, she was feeling distinctly mellow.

'Lovely!' she sighed happily. 'Oh, I did enjoy that. I shall forget all about diets for a few days.'

Philippa had taken off her jacket before dinner and Matthew's dark eyes travelled slowly and pleasurably over the curves beneath the navy crêpe blouse. 'Who said you should diet? You're just right as you are.' His voice was deep and lazy. His eyes held messages that were easy to interpret.

Philippa tried to pull herself together. She should

be resenting the way he was looking at her, but
instead she was enjoying it.

She lay back in her seat and closed her eyes. 'I
think,' she announced, 'that I shall pass the next few
hours sleeping.'

She heard Matthew's low chuckle again. 'I'll tell
the chef if I see him. He'll take that as a compliment!'

The big jumbo flew on steadily towards the North
Pole as Philippa slept, wakened, and slept again,
more soundly. She was finally awakened by a voice on
the intercom and the pressure of Matthew's hand on
her arm. 'Seat belt,' he told her. 'We'll be landing
shortly.'

'Oh—sorry,' she murmured, only half awake. She
fumbled to fasten the seat belt.

'Let me,' he said. She felt his hand touching her
waist, clicking the fastener, and she was suddenly
invaded by a swelling warmth inside herself. She
blinked herself awake. What was she thinking of? She
must be mad to let herself give in to these shamelessly
erotic sensations. Never since she had parted with
Gerald had she allowed any man to stimulate her, to
sense his power over her. But this man was dynamite.
She would have to be very, very careful, or she would
actually find herself feeling glad that he had taken
Adrian's place on the trip. And where would that get
her?

She sat up, putting a hand to her hair. 'Where are
we? What's happening?'

'We'll be coming in to land at Anchorage shortly,'
said Matthew, and that was what the voice on the
intercom must have been about. 'We can get out and
stretch our legs if you like.'

'Super.' Philippa was returning to full consciousness quickly now. 'A sniff of cold polar air is just what I need to waken me up.'

He laughed. 'I hope there won't be too much polar air in the transit lounge. I wouldn't advise leaping out on to the ice!'

The engine-note began to vary, Philippa felt a slight pressure on her ears, and then there was the sensation of touch-down. The engines shut off and the loudspeakers began to emit soothing music.

Philippa heard Matthew let out a long sigh. 'Nicely done,' he said as if he were complimenting the pilot personally, and she knew he had been nervous. That seemed to make him a little more human.

The doors were opened. 'Come along,' he said, speaking more quickly than usual. 'You can leave your holdall. Just put your jacket on and bring your handbag.'

Philippa looked for Sam as they made their way towards the transit lounge, but he wasn't visible among the crowd streaming along the grey, chilly corridor.

Matthew was just behind her as they reached the lounge. 'How do you fancy buying a fur coat?' His amused voice sounded in her ear. He had regained his poise—that little bit of it that had slipped. 'Or even a pair of fur earrings? You'll find them all over there.' His hand came round, pointing over her shoulder to the huddle of airport shops to their left.

'No, thanks, I'll settle for looking at the view.' Philippa turned towards the wide windows that ran along one side of the transit lounge. 'I think I'll—*Oh!*' She let out a yell as she came face to face with the most terrifying sight she had ever encountered. And stepped backwards straight into Matthew Vane's arms.

CHAPTER THREE

IT all happened in a flash—in that no-time in which accidents always happen. One moment she was standing petrified with terror; the next she was held tight in Matthew's arms, feeling a shock of realisation that what she had seen towering threateningly above her was a gigantic bear standing up on its back legs, quite eight feet of greyish-white menace, mouth open, fangs bared, eyes glaring, looking to Philippa for all the world as if it were just about to devour her. A polar bear. In a glass case.

She began to laugh shakily. 'Oh, I'm sorry—I wasn't expecting that—I——' She was shaking all over and she had never felt such a fool in her life.

Matthew kept his arms round her as he led her to a seat by the window, looking out over a bleak area of lowish mountains with patches of snow on them and dreary airport huts. The view did nothing to raise her spirits. She fumbled for a handkerchief and dabbed her eyes, half laughing, half crying. 'How idiotic of me—I'm so sorry——'

He sat down close beside her. 'Shut up, love,' he said softly. 'Just stay quiet.'

He was still holding her. She could feel the hard muscles in his arm, and her cheek was pressed against the thin smooth material of his jacket. And just for a moment she didn't want to draw away; she wanted him to go on holding her, wanted to feel safe and protected. Everything she had disliked about him up to now had faded away in this need to be held in his arms.

She dabbed her eyes again and sat up. What was she thinking of? She was a confident young career woman and this man was her boss. It wouldn't do her career much good if she collapsed into his arms at the sight of a stuffed bear.

'Hullo, what's up? Pippa feeling groggy?'

Sam was standing in front of them, Rex hovering behind.

Matthew got to his feet. 'Hullo, Sam—Rex. Philippa's fine now—just a touch of flying nerves. Stay and talk to her for a bit.'

He moved away across the lounge and Philippa watched him go. Watched his tall, straight back as he made his way between the groups of passengers towards the small complex of shops. And suddenly she was surprised by a strong feeling that she didn't want him to walk away from her. She drew in a deep, shaky breath as Sam sat down beside her and it was quite an effort to slip into the usual comradely office patter.

'Hullo, Sam. How's everything?'

'Fine,' he said. 'Everything's fine.' He looked closely at her. 'Are you all right, Pippa? You look very pale.'

She smiled at him. 'Recovering fast. I'm rather a novice in this jet-setting league.' She didn't want to explain about the bear.

'Me too,' Sam admitted. 'But they tell me flying's safer than crossing the road, so I keep reminding myself of all the statistics that prove it. I listed them before we left.' He pulled out a length of computer print-out. 'Look, we're in the "better than world average class".

Philippa studied the long strip of paper and laughed. 'Oh, Sam, you think everything's solved by computer, don't you?'

He tucked the print-out away in his pocket. 'Most things are, or will be. Soon we'll be able to tell them our intimate problems and get the answer from them.'

'The marriage-guidance computer—it's a nice thought.' Philippa kept a straight face.

'O.K., you can mock, young Philippa, but I bet most couples would rather talk about their sex life to a computer than to a social worker.'

'It won't concern you, will it, Sam dear, as you're already married to one—a computer, I mean, of course,' Philippa teased, and he raised a hand in warning.

Rex had wandered away while this cheerful exchange had been going on and was lighting up a cigarette in a far corner of the room. Matthew had disappeared altogether. Philippa said, 'Are you—comfortable on the flight, Sam?'

He blinked at her through his large spectacles. 'Comfortable? Yes, it's fine—why?'

'I just wondered—I feel rather bad about travelling first-class. I didn't know about it until we actually boarded the plane. I'd much rather we'd been all together.'

'Oh, I think it's better as it is,' Sam told her easily. 'Rex and I might not know the right knives and forks to use when dining with the Top People.'

'Sam, you *are* an idiot,' protested Philippa. 'But I just wanted you to know that it's none of my doing. Matthew Vane says it wasn't his doing either, that

Adrian booked the flights that way.'

Sam threw her a quick glance. 'That's probably true. I'm pretty sure he'd have booked first-class for himself.'

'But not for me,' Philippa insisted.

Sam gave her an old-fashioned look. 'Wouldn't he, though? Well, Matt Vane's getting the benefit anyway, and I bet he's enjoying the company.' Sam's eyes twinkled and, to her discomfiture, Philippa found herself flushing.

'I'd still rather be with you and Rex,' she insisted.

Sam grinned. 'Ah, make the most of it, Pippa, and enjoy all the luvly grub.' He rolled his eyes. 'They give you free champagne first-class, don't they? Me, I prefer beer.'

Rex strolled up, ripping open a cigarette packet, and a moment later Matthew joined them from the direction of the shops. He, too, had a packet in his hand, but it wasn't cigarettes. 'Macadamia nuts,' he said, handing it round. 'Chocolate-covered. A speciality here—help yourselves, see how you like them.'

While they all munched nuts and chatted Philippa was watching Matthew. His attitude towards the two men—and towards herself if it came to that—was different from his attitude back in the office in England. Easier, less autocratic. Evidently he had calculated that it would benefit him—and the success of the trip—if he unbent a little. She couldn't believe that he had suddenly become more friendly and sociable.

She found herself watching him all the time. She needed to study him, she told herself, if she were to notice anything about him that roused her suspicions, but anyone less like the villian of the classic detective stories she enjoyed it would have been difficult to find. The real villian invariably puts the reader off the scent by being all sweetness and light. Matthew Vane could hardly have conformed less to that pattern, even though he was putting on a good act with Sam and Rex at the moment. She assured herself that it *was* an act. Already she judged Matthew Vane as a man who did nothing on impulse—every act of his would be calculated.

She felt that she was beginning to understand the man a little; that would help her to be on her guard against the strong physical magnetism that she had already encountered.

The call came through to rejoin the plane and he turned to her, where she sat, and smiled and held out a hand. 'O.K., Philippa? Recovered?'

She could hardly not take the hand he offered, but as it closed round her own hand and he drew her to her feet her knees went weak and a thrill ran through her body like a jagged lightning flash. For a crazy moment she expected him to pull her close, to take her in his arms.

'Don't forget your handbag,' he said, and she looked down stupidly to see that she had left it on the seat.

Sam and Rex had gone on ahead. 'That bear really has something to answer for,' Matthew said amusedly.

Philippa paused before the great threatening beast as they passed, and glared up at it. 'I'm not afraid of you,' she told it. 'You're just a great big fraud!'

The bear was dead, he couldn't hurt her unless she let her imagination run riot. But there were other dangers, and it was as well to keep a tight curb on her imagination. She looked up at the man beside her and he looked down and smiled at her and there were crinkles beside his eyes. Yes, there were certainly other dangers.

When they were settled back in their seats Matthew felt in his pocket and drew out a package. 'A small memento of the trip.' He handed it to her.

'For me? How kind,' Philippa said politely, pulling off the wrapping paper, expecting more nuts, or sweets of some kind. Inside a decorated box was a small polar-bear fur brooch.

'Oh, how absolutely marevellous!' She held the perfect little object in her hand. 'Thank you.'

'You might call it a "hair of the bear",' Matthew said gravely.

She nodded. 'I'll never be scared by a polar bear again,' she said.

'Nor by anything else, I hope.' He wasn't smiling. 'Let me pin it on for you; it goes well with your suit.'

She felt his hand touch her breast as he pinned the brooch in place and there it was again—the thrill rippling through her. She held her breath; it would go in a moment.

'There,' he said. 'It looks good.' He could have let his hand linger on her breast, but he hadn't. Of course he hadn't. He wasn't a man to start anything with a junior girl in his own firm. He had merely relaxed his office persona sufficiently to be friendly. He couldn't help being wildly sexy, she supposed, it was something you were born with, like thick dark hair and absurdly long lashes and high cheekbones that threw shadows on to lean cheeks. No, so long as she didn't go completely overboard and throw herself into his arms, she wouldn't have anything to fear from him on the trip.

'Thank you for not giving me away to Sam about the polar bear,' she said. 'He's a great tease and I should never have heard the last of it if he'd known about my idiocy.'

'And thank you, too,' he said gravely.

She turned huge blue eyes on him. 'What for?'

'For not commenting on my passing weakness. You realised I was scared stiff when we landed, didn't you?'

'Yes, well, I thought——'

'I always am, I don't get over it. Like most people who enjoy driving I'm a God-awful passenger.'

'You mean you're a pilot yourself?'

He nodded. 'In a small way. Just one of the amateurs who like to fantasise about taking the controls of Concorde.' He smiled and changed the subject. 'You get on well with Sam, do you?'

'Oh yes, Sam's a dear, and delightful to work for—except that he never knows when to stop working,' she grimaced.

'And with Rex?'

Philippa hesitated. 'Rex is a very nice man, I'm sure of it, but not the sort you get to know. He's very friendly, though.' Matthew probably knew all about Rex's problems, but if not she wasn't going to mention them.

The hours passed. Flying west they were following the sun, so there was light for a long time. Matthew seemed absorbed in his papers, except for the times that meals were served when he roused himself to become an amusing host. Stewardesses hovered, attending to their every want, offering drinks, snacks. A film flickered on the screen at the end of the cabin, but Philippa snuggled down so that the back of the seat in front hid it from her view. She didn't feel like watching an American comedy. She was glad when darkness came and the cabin lights were dimmed, and the ever-solicitous stewardesses laid rugs over their knees.

Matthew stowed his papers and laid back his head and was almost immediately asleep. Philippa snuggled under the soft rug and closed her eyes, but sleep wouldn't come. Perhaps it was because she kept opening her eyes again to look at the sleeping man beside her. It was a very odd experience, he looked so much younger, almost vulnerable in sleep. In fact, the whole journey was turning out very odd indeed. Perhaps things would seem more normal when they got to Japan.

From the moment they reached Tokyo Matthew was in charge. 'Right,' he said, once his small team had gathered together in the main concourse of the great international airport. 'Programme for the day.'

He looked at his watch. 'Ten-thirty, Tokyo time. First we book in at the hotel where Philippa and I are staying. We leave Philippa there—no point in trailing her round with us—and then the three of us will go along to the travel office and find out exactly what arrangements have been made for you and Rex, Sam. I gather you two have been booked in at a hotel nearer to the place where they're putting on the trade fair. I want to make sure you have a guide and interpreter booked. You know the drill, Sam, don't you? You'll spend tomorrow at the trade fair and the following day you'll visit the Works and get a general idea how they do things here. I think you'll find everyone very helpful, and I also guess that you'll be bowled over by the super way the Japanese run their industries. While you two are, so to speak, at the cutting edge I shall make my contacts at administration level. We'll be in touch by phone every evening. Right? Come on then, let's get going. We can take a Limousine bus to the city air terminal—it's probably quicker than trying to find a taxi.'

As the bus glided smoothly along the expressway Philippa stared out of the window at flat fields, rather scrubby wooded areas and low, dun-coloured houses, and tried to adjust to the programme that Matthew had just outlined. It was an unpleasant surprise to discover that their party was going to split up and that Sam and Rex would be staying in a different hotel.

She would be alone with Matthew then—a pair, a couple; which was a very different thing from being two of a team of four, as she had expected. She mustn't be naïve and silly about it, she told herself. This was a business trip and she was a business girl—cool, confident, quite capable of making decisions about her personal life. She had no real reason to suppose that Matthew would expect anything from her except that she do her job efficiently. But—a man travelling abroad with his secretary! The very idea seemed to carry overtones. She would have to be on her guard.

At the terminal they took a taxi to the hotel and now they passed through what was evidently the central part of the city, with shops and department stores, glittering and glamorous, hung with colourful banner-like signs inscribed from top to bottom in Japanese characters. Glossy cars glided along, filling the streets. The pavements were crowded; men in dark suits, girls in smart outfits walked purposefully. No lounging about, as one saw in London or Birmingham. Life appeared to be proceeding at a faster rate, and yet everything seemed to be orderly, organised. It all looked clean and spruce. This was the Tokyo that Philippa had read about and recognised from pictures in her books, and as they passed a park and the Tokyo Tower she began to feel her spirits rising. She wouldn't let anything spoil her enjoyment of being in this new, vastly interesting place.

But there was nothing Oriental that Philippa could see about the huge hotel when they reached it; it seemed completely Westernised. Matthew settled her in the lounge with a tray of coffee and then she said goodbye to Sam and Rex before they were borne off again.

'Wait here till I get back,' was Matthew's parting instruction, 'I don't want to lose you,' and she must have been imagining the ever-so-slightly intimate flavour he gave to the words. Don't go meeting trouble halfway, she told herself, and managed to relax and enjoy the experience of sitting back and sipping her coffee while she watched the people who passed ceaselessly through the lounge. Japanese, mostly, but there was a sprinkling of Europeans and Americans as well. She made a game of guessing their nationalities.

When Matthew slipped into the seat beside her she was so relaxed that her eyelids were drooping and she felt on the verge of sleep. She sat up immediately. 'You've been quick,' she said.

He smiled and signalled to a passing waiter to bring more coffee. 'I've been well over an hour as it happens.'

'Oh, goodness, I must have been asleep.' She rubbed her eyes.

'Reasonable,' he said. 'It's about three o'clock in the morning, according to your body, at which time most people are fast asleep in bed. Have some more coffee, that'll help you wake up. And if you like you can kip down for a couple of hours to catch up, when we get our sleeping arrangements sorted out.'

'Oh no, thanks, I'll wake up soon,' she said, as the waiter brought coffee on a lacquer tray. She poured it out for them both. 'Did you get Sam and Rex fixed up?'

'Yes, quite satisfactorily. Your Adrian did a good job of making bookings and reservations.'

Philippa couldn't let that pass. 'He isn't *my* Adrian.'

'No?' His dark brows rose, his mouth took on a wry twist.

She changed the subject quickly. 'I didn't know that Sam and Rex weren't going to be staying at the hotel with us.'

'That's the way Adrian Banks arranged it,' he said smoothly, sipping his coffee. 'Does it bother you?'

'No, of course not, only—only I like to know what's going on.' She had a sudden urge to get things straight. 'At the moment I feel like an actress who suddenly finds herself on the stage in the wrong play, and doesn't know any of the lines.'

He laughed, not unkindly. 'Poor Philippa—never mind, you just stay close to me and I'll feed you all the right cues.' He put down his coffee cup. 'For a start, let's see what accommodation Banks has booked for us. You wait here with the bags.'

She watched him disappear round the corner towards the reception desk and a few minutes later a smiling Japanese boy in a smart uniform collected their bags and escorted them up to the twenty-third floor, unlocked a door, placed their bags within and departed, bowing deeply.

A glance around told Philippa that this was an ordinary, Western-style hotel bedroom, well equipped and comfortable, with a large double bed. The only Japanese touch seemed to be two cotton robes laid out on the bed and two pairs of slippers beside it.

Matthew strolled across to the window. 'Good view,' he mused, looking down. 'You can see across to Tokushima Park—there's a zoo there, I was taken to visit it last time I came to Japan.'

Philippa was staring at the double bed. 'Is this my room or yours?' she asked Matthew's back.

He turned round, glanced about the room as if he hadn't really noticed it before, and said, 'Ours, I gather. That was how friend Banks booked it.' He strolled across and stood before her and there was something very intimidating in his size, at close quarters. 'Don't pretend you're surprised, Philippa,' he said quietly.

'Of course I'm surprised!' she burst out angrily. 'I'd never intended to share a room with Adrian and he knew it!'

From the way he smiled she knew he didn't believe her. 'Do I take it, then, that you wouldn't consider sharing a room with me?'

'Of course I wouldn't. I hardly know you.'

'I could rectify that very quickly.'

'No,' she said again.

He sank down into a cane chair and leaned back, his hands linked behind his head, regarding her closely as she stood beside the dressing fitment, her back stiff, her chin raised, every inch of her registering determination.

'You're ambitious, are you, Philippa? You want to get ahead in the company?'

Taken unaware, she replied quickly, 'Yes, of course. I want——' Then, too late, she caught the drift of his question and added, blue eyes gleaming frostily, 'But not by sleeping my way to the top, if that's what you're suggesting.'

'"Just an idea,' he said amiably. 'It seems pretty obvious that that was what Adrian Banks had in mind. No—' he raised a hand as she opened her mouth to deny it again '——for the moment I'm prepared to accept your word that he was rushing things somewhat. Rather a clumsy way to go about it. For myself,' he went on very smoothly, 'I don't care to rush things. You've read about Japanese Zen, have you?'

'A little,' Philippa admitted dubiously. What was he getting at?

'I like the Zen way of tackling things. Take the way they learn archery, for instance. They spend time—days, weeks, as long as it takes—just getting everything right: the place, the bow, the arrow, themselves—mind and body. But they never actually shoot the arrow. They just wait and when the moment arrives, the arrow shoots itself. And it always flies straight to the target.'

He stood up. 'End of lecture. More another time.' He smiled at her. 'Meanwhile I shall go down to

Reception and demand—no, not demand, the Japanese appreciate politeness—I shall *request* another room.' He strolled to the door. 'See you soon.'

Philippa sank on to the bed. What an odd conversation! But everything about the trip had been odd, as she had noticed on the plane. Matthew had probably been right about Adrian's intentions, and that annoyed her because it gave Matthew the wrong impression. Still, he had accepted her word and gone off to book a separate room, and that was a relief.

But what on earth had he meant by his little story about the arrow and the target? What a strange, unexpected, and—yes, admit it, fascinating man he was!

She sat on the bed feeling rather lost in the impersonal hotel room. She hadn't realised that the hotels in Japan could be quite so Westernised. She had read about Japanese inns, *ryokans* they were called, where Westerners could sometimes stay, but this was a business trip, not a tourist holiday, so she supposed she wouldn't be able to get much of a flavour of the real Japan. Matthew had promised to introduce her to Japanese cooking, so that would have to do.

He seemed to be away a long time and when he came back he turned down both thumbs expressively. 'No go,' he said. 'They've got two big conventions on here at present and they're booked solid. The only suggestion they can make is that we exchange this room for a small suite which we can have for a couple of nights. One of the men at the convention had booked it for himself and his wife, but the wife hasn't been able to come. They managed to contact him and he's willing to do the swap—probably he'd save some cash on it. So that's what I've arranged. I've seen the suite—it's three floors below—and there's a sort of divan thing in the sitting-room that I can sleep on. I'm afraid we'll have to share the bathroom. O.K.? Does that satisfy your maidenly modesty?'

Philippa said coldly, 'You're making a huge joke of all this, but I really don't think it's very funny.'

'Perhaps not funny, but not a big serious thing either.'

'That's a matter of opinion,' she said. 'Couldn't we move to another hotel?'

Suddenly his expression changed. He was once more the high-handed Matthew Vane of the office back in Britain. 'You don't know what you're talking about, girl,' he said curtly. 'It's pretty sure all the hotels are booked solid, with these conventions on. And anyway, this one suits me. There are special facilities laid on for visiting business executives that you might not get elsewhere.' He glared at her as she seemed about to speak. 'Now, just pipe down and make the best of it, that's a good girl. I've no intention of seducing you, if that's what's on your little mind.'

At that moment the porter arrived, smiling and bowing, to escort them to their new quarters and, short of making a big fuss, there was nothing that Philippa could do about it. But she was seething with annoyance as they went down in the lift. Annoyance with Matthew Vane for being so pompous, but mostly annoyance with herself for having begun to allow her opinion of him to soften and mellow. He really was a chauvinistic beast, just as she'd first thought.

He might say, in his nasty putting-down way, that

he had no intention of seducing her, but he would have had no scruples about sharing a bed with her if she had been willing. How could she possibly know what would happen in the next days?

Philippa wasn't a girl for casual sex—never had been. She had been in love with Gerald, deep in love, and bitterly unhappy and humiliated at the ending of the affair. Since Gerald there had been nobody special and she had shied away from anything intimate. Adrian had been different—friendly, undemanding. She had begun to wonder if she would, perhaps, fall in love with him. But if Matthew Vane were to be believed she had been mistaken in Adrian too.

Perhaps, she thought wryly, as they got out of the lift, I'm just a poor judge of men. All the more reason to keep her distance from Matthew.

The suite was quite luxurious, more so than the double room they had been shown into before. When the young porter had gone Matthew carried Philippa's bag into the bedroom and dumped it on the bed. He looked round. 'Satisfied now?' he said curtly.

She had to keep her end up or Matthew Vane would push her around unmercifully. She said coolly, 'I would have preferred to have a room entirely separate, but I realise that this is the best that could be managed.'

He glared at her. 'Hell!' he exploded. 'You don't seem to appreciate that I've gone to a lot of trouble to go along with your coy, virtuous play-acting, my girl. You're not the modest violet type, not with that hair and those eyes. And don't try to make me believe that you weren't willing to share a room with Adrian Banks—or at the very least that you'd led him on to expect that. Remember, I saw you coming down from his bedroom at the Lord Leycester in Warwick, looking very much the worse for wear.'

Oh no, she wasn't going to take this from him—no way! Her eyes flashed blue fire as she faced up to him. 'Look, Mr Vane, my relationship with Adrian has nothing at all to do with you. I'm not working for Adrian on this trip, I'm working for you, and unless you're prepared to treat me with—with respect I would like to hand in my resignation. Presumably there's a return ticket booked for me, and I'm sure you can get along without my services here.'

To her utter chagrin she saw that he was laughing when she finished her little speech. 'Oh, Philippa, I do like you when you're angry!' He came across the room and put his hands on her shoulders and gave her a little shake. 'I felt sure there was some way to get the adrenalin flowing.'

She gasped. 'You've been baiting me, you're just a beastly chauvinist!'

'Not really—at least not beastly, I hope.' He shook his head solemnly. 'I needed to find out what was under that attractive exterior. I might have found out in the normal course of events, but we only have a few days together and I couldn't wait.'

'So—you've summed me up, have you?' she grated through clenched teeth. 'I'd be fascinated to hear your conclusions.'

'I'm sure you would, but at the moment I'll keep my conclusions to myself. There is one thing I'll tell you, though—Adrian Banks isn't the man for you. It's just as well I brought you along with me.'

Her eyes searched his face to find the meaning behind this extraordinary pronouncement, but his expression told her nothing.

'You mean,' she said at last, slowly, incredulously, 'you brought me on this trip to get me away from Adrian? Why? Why does it concern you?'

He smiled hatefully. 'Oh, I don't like to see a nice girl throwing herself away on a man who wouldn't be any good to her.'

This was getting more and more fantastic by the minute. 'You don't really expect me to believe that, do you?' His hands were still on her shoulders and while he touched her there was a strong current flowing between the two of them—no use denying it. Exactly what emotion was making it flow she wasn't prepared to decide. Dislike? Contempt? Just pure anger, perhaps? 'And will you please take your hands off me!' she snapped, and was mortified to hear how her voice shook.

His hands were clamped more firmly on her shoulders and he went on as if she hadn't spoken. 'Adrian Banks could never satisfy a girl like you, not a girl with your gorgeous hair, and eyes that speak volumes.' He was looking thoughtfully into her face and his own eyes were so liquid dark, with their long, thick lashes, so devastatingly magnetic that she couldn't manage to look away. The current between them was flowing more strongly than ever—sweeping her along somewhere, she didn't know where.

'And,' he added softly, 'you've got six freckles on the bridge of your nose. I never could resist freckles.'

His face came nearer and Philippa held her breath. She ought to resist, pull away, fight him, but her body was limp. His mouth lowered itself and brushed the bridge of her nose backwards and

forwards gently. Then it slid down and closed over
her mouth, as his hands lowered to her waist,
holding her lightly against him.

It wasn't a sensual kiss, not deliberately disturbing; it was rather as if he were asking her a question,
and it was over almost before it had begun, but when
he lifted his mouth her knees felt like elastic and her
pulses were hammering.

He held her away from him, smiling. 'There, that
was a kiss of peace. Can we be friends now Philippa?
I'm sorry if you objected to my underhand methods.
But please don't talk about leaving me. I really shall
need your help, you know, and I've had very good
reports of your work.'

She pulled away and sat down on the nearest
seat—which was the bed. How did you cope with a
man like this? One moment bawling her out, then
indulging in a brief but highly-charged flirtation,
and finally returning to the cool businesslike ap-
proach that was what she expected—and wanted.

Or did she?

She wasn't sure. She wasn't sure of anything any
longer.

How did that old song go? *Bewitched, bothered and
bewildered*. That just about summed it up.

CHAPTER FOUR

'NOW that we've got that fixed up we'll organise ourselves,' Matthew announced. He dropped his travelling-bag on the bed and zipped it open. 'As I said, I'll sleep in the sitting-room next door, but we don't want to fill it up in the daytime with all my clobber.' He walked across and slid open the white-painted door of the clothes closet. 'Tasteful, don't you agree? The Japanese manage to set their own individual touch to things.' He waved a hand towards the spray of cherry blossom painted on one corner of the large door.

'Very tasteful,' Philippa agreed stiffly. She had understood that she was going to have her own bedroom, but it looked as if Matthew would be in and out every time he wanted a clean shirt or another handkerchief.

He slid a glance her way and took a knitted cashmere shirt from his bag, making heavy weather of pushing it on to a hanger, until Philippa could stand it no longer. 'Here, let me do it.' She took it from him, folded it and put it in a drawer. 'You shouldn't hang knitted garments up,' she said, remembering Gran's teaching. 'It pulls them out of shape.'

He grimaced. 'How should I know? I never had a wife to instruct me in these niceties. You'd better do the rest of my unpacking for me.' He pulled off his shoes and settled himself on the bed, crossing his long legs in front of him.

73

She regarded him coldly. 'Is that an order—sir?'

He chuckled. 'Yes, it is.'

Tight-lipped, Philippa began to do as she was told. She supposed this might be construed as a personal secretary's job, but as she hadn't been trained as a secretary she wouldn't know.

Matthew's organising ability certainly didn't extend to his packing, which was extremely haphazard. Shirts were rolled up rather than folded, shoes were stacked on top, socks and handkerchiefs stuffed into them. Shaving gear was wrapped round with several pairs of cotton Y-fronts. There was no sign of pyjamas. Philippa felt her colour rising as she gritted her teeth and finished stacking everything away, arranging brushes on the dressing-chest and toiletries on the shelf in the adjoining small bathroom. It really wasn't on, she thought resentfully, he shouldn't expect her to do this—this intimate job for him. It made it worse that he should have been lounging there watching her with an amused smile on his face.

'There.' She closed a drawer with unnecessary force. 'That's the lot.'

'Excellent,' he said. 'Very capably done. You'll make some lucky fellow a good wife, Philippa.'

'Thank you.' She unzipped her own bag with an abrupt swish. 'As I've no intention of getting married for a long, long time—if ever—the question doesn't arise.'

'Really? Now that does surprise me.' He thought for a moment. 'You're not—you haven't been—married, have you?'

'No, I haven't. I'd have thought you'd have found that out when you went through my personal particulars back at the office. Before you decided that you wanted to bring me here as your *personal secretary*.' She turned and leaned back against the dressing-chest. 'And while I think of it, why exactly *did* you bring me? Why couldn't you have brought a real secretary—your own, or one of the girls from the general office?'

'You really want to know?' He eyed her lazily.

'Yes, I do. I still can't see what use I'm going to be to you.'

He grinned—a wicked, sexy grin. He hadn't smiled at her like that before and it took her by surprise. Something warm and disturbing fluttered in the region of her stomach. 'I can think of several uses you might be to me,' he drawled. 'A business trip like this doesn't have to be all work, and it's pleasant to have an attractive companion. And none of the other girls is nearly as pretty as you are, Philippa.'

Before she could pull herself together and think of a reply that would take the smile off his face, he consulted his watch, swung his legs off the bed and began to put his shoes on again. 'But less of this frivolity, there's work to do. Now I suggest that you have a rest here and get over your jet-lag while I go out and pay a courtesy call at the office of our good friends—the ones we shall be meeting with tomorrow. The Japanese are very formal about these things and hate to be taken by surprise. They'll be expecting Adrian Banks, of course, and I must advise them of the change. Just have a look in my briefcase and see if you can find some business cards. I put them in one of the pockets.'

'Are these what you mean?' Philippa pulled out a

stack of cards. Very impressive cards they were, too. The name of the company in large letters, top left. In the left bottom corner, Matthew M. Vane, Director. On the right side, from top to bottom were inscribed Japanese symbols.

'Beautiful,' she mused, with her back to him. She loved the Japanese script and wished she could understand even a few words of it.

Matthew tied his second shoelace and stood up. 'Beautiful, I agree.' He was looking at her, not the card. 'Your hair is fantastic, I can't get over it.' He took a handful of the silky coppery fall of hair and let it slide through his fingers. 'Fantastic!' he murmured again softly.

At the touch of his hand on her neck the warm disturbance began again in the pit of her stomach. She was dizzily sure that in a moment his arms would come round her from behind and pull her against him. She stood very still, waiting for it to happen, willing it to happen. She must have gone mad, she thought. Quite, quite mad.

But instead Matthew reached round her to pick up one of the brushes that she had set out, and leaned to the mirror, raking the brush vigorously through his dark hair. He selected a green tie with a discreet pattern and knotted it. Then he took up a clothes brush and held it out to Philippa. 'Thanks,' he said, obviously expecting her to use it.

She flicked the brush over the shoulders of his jacket. 'Is this the job of a personal secretary too?' she enquired stiffly.

'The job of a personal secretary, my girl, is to do anything and everything to make life smoother for her boss.'

He picked up the stack of cards, handed one to her and tucked the rest away in an inside pocket. 'You'd better keep one of these on you. It's always wise to have an easy positive identification when in a foreign country.'

Obediently she put the card into her handbag. 'I hope I shan't be kidnapped, or run over by a bus.' She wished she could make some witty remark, but everything she said sounded flip and silly. She wanted quite desperately to feel easy with him, to talk naturally as she would do with Sam, with Adrian, with any of the men she met. But instead she felt stiff and stupid.

'You won't be, I'll see to that.' His eyes held hers and she had a crazy feeling that his arms were round her, protecting her.

She laughed shakily. 'It sounds as if I'm going to be more of a drag than a help to you!'

'Oh, I'll make you work when the need arises.' He spoke absently now, he was sorting through the papers in his briefcase, checking that everything was there that he would need.

'Matt——' Philippa ventured. She must practise using his first name, as he wished, but it felt awkward.

'Um?' He didn't look up.

'Matt, what exactly are we doing here? Nobody has told me. I know I'm only a very small cog in a big wheel, but it would help if I had some idea what was going on.'

He looked up quickly then. 'Didn't Banks tell you? I'd have thought he would have taken you into his confidence.' His eyes narrowed, fixed on her keenly. He seemed, for some reason that she

couldn't fathom, to be waiting for her answer with
great interest.

When she shook her head he shrugged. 'No? Well,
I'm afraid I haven't got time now. Later on, perhaps.
Now, have a rest and wait here until I come back.
The office I have to visit is in the Mananouchi
district, that's the business part of the city, and I
have to locate the office—not the easiest thing to do
in Tokyo—so I may be some time. Right?'

He didn't wait for her reply. The door closed
behind him before she could draw breath to make
one.

Philippa slumped down on to the bed, all the
energy drained out of her, and let her hands rest
beside her on the heavy-patterned bedcover. She
could feel the warmth where Matt had just been
sitting. He had gone, but the whole room was still
full of his powerful masculine presence.

When he was with her she found it difficult to
hang on to the self-image she had built up slowly and
painfully over the year after her break with Gerald.
Never again, she had vowed, would she let herself be
swayed by the sensuality of an attractive man. She
believed that she knew all about her body's physical
reactions—the inner churning, the sudden weakness
that made your knees tremble, the warmth that crept
through your body making it soft and languid. Oh
yes, she had known that, and now she wouldn't trust
it ever again.

Matthew Vane issued a sexual challenge just by
existing. His broad shoulders, lean hips, strong
thighs, the curve of his mouth, the slight droop of
lids over glittering dark eyes. The lithe movements,
aloof raising of his brows, the way his face could

harden suddenly or break into a smile that tugged at your inside—oh yes, he had the lot. He was a winner in the sex stakes.

But Philippa wasn't competing in any sex stakes, and she had every intention of ignoring the way her body reacted to him. She recognised and admitted that the strong attraction was there, and knowing the danger was half the battle won, she told herself. There was no future in letting herself fall in love again—with someone like Matthew Vane.

She got up quickly and occupied herself unpacking her own bag. The two light dresses had travelled beautifully and she hung them in the closet, together with her white corduroy showercoat, pushing them to the far end of the rail from Matt's shirts and spare trousers. On the dressing-chest she arranged her own brushes at the opposite side from his, with her small make-up box and bottles of perfume spray behind them.

She stared down at the two separate groups of brushes, pots and bottles. This was how it would be to live with a man. Two of everything, but two that made a pair inside a loving relationship. To share things—a room, a wardrobe, a dressing-table, a bed.

A bed. She felt the colour rise into her cheeks. She was becoming more and more certain that Matthew was expecting her to share his bed, whatever he said about having no intention of seducing her. Everything pointed to it. And had he really done the best he could in booking this suite instead of providing her with a separate room? She had no way of finding out—but she doubted it.

She crossed the room and examined the door that led into the sitting-room. No lock. She shrugged. Oh well, she would just have to deal with any situation that arose, but if Matthew Vane thought she would tamely agree to amuse him when his beautiful girl-friend, Heidi, wasn't on the scene, he was very mistaken!

She swilled her face and hands and renewed her make-up. What to do now? Rest, he had said, but she had never felt less like resting. Wait here for me, he had said, but why should she? The room was air-conditioned, but what she longed for, after all those hours of air-conditioning in the plane, was a breath of fresh air. Of course she wouldn't go roaming about Tokyo on her own, that would be pure stupidity. But there was nothing to stop her from going down in the lift and out of the front door and taking a look around. She went out and shut the door, putting the key in her handbag.

She found the express lift and was whizzed down to the ground floor. The row of lifts opened into the lounge and she started to walk through it to the entrance foyer. Her one thought was to get to the open air and she walked briskly. Then she stopped dead, catching her breath. At a table in the far corner of the lounge, half hidden behind a pillar, sat Matthew, in close conversation with another man, a dark-suited Japanese, with black glossy hair and enormous spectacles. Matthew had his back half-turned to her and it was unlikely that he would see her from where she stood, but in order to reach the front entrance she would have to pass within a few yards of the table where he was sitting.

She didn't stop to think out what he would do or say if he saw her walking out of the hotel. She found herself back in the lift and ascending to the twentieth floor before she really knew what she was doing.

In the suite she sank into a chair, breathing hard. Why she had run away like that she didn't really know. It would have been the simplest thing in the world to explain to Matthew that she was going outside for a breath of air, if he had questioned her. But there was something about the way he had been talking to that man—leaning acros the table, chin on hand. Something almost—furtive?—about it. And they looked as if they had been sitting there for ages. Certainly there hadn't been time for him to travel to an office in another district, transact his business there and get back again and now be here talking in the lounge. Was this what Adrian had meant when he asked her to keep an eye on Matthew and note anything even vaguely suspicious in his conduct? Philippa twisted her fingers together, feeling cold and miserable. She was utterly out of her depth here—with Matthew Vane and with the whole situation. She should never have agreed to come.

'Hullo—I thought you were going to lie down and rest.' Philippa jumped as Matthew's voice came from behind her. She hadn't heard him come in—he must have opened the door very quietly.

His sudden appearance had made her heart race. 'I felt more like a shower and a change of clothes.' She tried to sound offhand. 'Did you find your contacts at the office you were going to?'

He gave her a strange look. 'Contacts? Oh yes, of course.'

Philippa concentrated on unpacking the oddments at the bottom of her bag. 'Was it as far away as you thought—the office, I mean? Did it take you long to get there?'

She spoke idly—a throwaway question, hardly requiring a serious answer. But she had to know if he would lie to her. She had to find out something of the character of the man she was dealing with. Could he possibly be the kind of man who would defraud the company he owed his loyalty to? She found she didn't want to believe it.

She heard a sharp click as he locked his briefcase. Then, slowly, he came across the room and stood looking down at her, and there was a strange glint in his dark eyes. 'As a matter of fact, I haven't been out.'

'Oh,' she said blankly. 'Oh—haven't you?' So he hadn't lied to her. The rush of relief she felt was alarming.

His eyes were still fixed on her with that searching look. 'You know very well that I haven't, don't you Philippa? You saw me down in the lounge and calculated that I hadn't been out at all. Then you tried to catch me out about it. *Why?*'

Her mouth was suddenly dry. 'I didn't—I only thought——'

She realised that he wasn't listening to her. The report she had made for Adrian was at the bottom of her open bag, which was lying beside her on the dressing-stool, and Matthew was looking down at it, dark brows drawn into a frown. 'What's this?' He reached into her bag and pulled out the sheaf of papers.

'Oh, it's not important now, just some notes I made. I thought they might be useful.' She had made the report for Adrian, sitting up late at nights combing the pages of the *Financial Times* for anything that was going on in Japan in their own line of business.

'H'm.' Matthew's frown deepened as he flicked over the pages. 'And whose benefit was this for?

Adrian Banks's, I suppose?'

'Well, yes, in the first instance.' Her cheeks were beginning to burn under his dark scrutiny. 'I thought he might be able to make use of it.'

'I bet he would! Too bad he isn't here to reap the benefit of all this painstaking work.' His glance was ironic now, his mouth a hard, straight line. 'I'll keep this, I think.' He opened his briefcase and slipped the document in. 'It might come in handy.'

'Oh, I hope so,' said Philippa. 'I'd hate to think I'd wasted all that time and effort.' She had intended to sound as ironic as he, but to her dismay the words sounded merely flippant.

She moved towards the sitting-room—anywhere to get away from that dark, frowning gaze—but as she reached the door his voice arrested her. 'Philippa.'

She turned, one hand on the door-knob. He walked across the room to her. 'You're very friendly with Adrian Banks, aren't you?' He loomed above her. When he came as close as this her knees began to go weak.

'Well—yes, I suppose so. We get on well together. But I seem to get on well with everyone at the branch. They're all very easy and friendly.'

He smiled thinly. 'With one notable exception?'

She met the dark eyes and somehow managed a cool little smile herself. 'You said it, Mr Vane.'

For what seemed a very long time their glances locked and Philippa would not—could not—look away. She wanted to step backwards but she was close up against the door, which he had left ajar when he came in.

Now he put his hands out either side of her and

pushed the door to. 'A warning,' he said, his voice very low.

'Oh dear, what have I done now?' Again that awful flippancy—she could have kicked herself.

'I'm not quite sure—yet,' he said slowly. 'But I'm just warning you. Don't play games with me, Philippa. You wouldn't have a hope of winning, you know.'

She felt a shiver pass through her. There was a hard note in the deep voice that seemed to spell danger, more like a threat than a warning. She stared up at him with huge, alarmed blue eyes.

'I—I don't know what you mean,' she stammered.

'I hope you don't,' he said darkly. 'I prefer us to be working on the same side.'

Then, suddenly, his mood changed. He laughed and linked an arm with hers. 'Now come along, let's look for a coffee-shop—I'm hungry! And later on I've got some work for you to do. They're sending up an electronic typewriter, so you'll be able to get busy.'

The coffee-shop was a disappointment to Philippa. Except for the wall decorations of leaves, fans, and birds, and the garlands of plastic flowers draped from the ceiling of the bar, they might almost have been back in England. They sat on high stools and ate hamburgers and drank coffee, and she looked around at the busy, crowded room, frowning slightly.

'Food not to your liking?' Matt enquired, with his ironic grin.

'The food? Oh yes, the food's fine. I was just thinking——'

'Yes?'

'It seems odd that here we are in the middle of an ancient Oriental city with its own customs and traditions, and yet all these very Japanese-looking people seem quite happy eating hamburgers and hot-dogs and pizzas.'

'Ah, I see. You were expecting geishas and kimonos and chopsticks and all that stuff?'

'Yes, I suppose I was.' Philippa pulled a wry face. 'Very naïve, of me.'

He looked at her steadily. 'I don't think you're naïve, Philippa. I just wonder if——' He broke off. 'Oh, never mind. But as far as your expectations are concerned we must make sure that you see something of the old Japan before we leave, and not just offices and American-style coffee-shops.'

'Oh, please don't feel——' Philippa began hastily. 'I know I'm here on a business trip. I don't expect——'

'Ssh!' He reached out and covered her hand with his, and his touch sent messages tingling up and down her spine. 'Business trips are not always taken up exclusively with business. There are other things—quite important things——'

'Oh yes?' Philippa murmured warily, and held her breath. She thought she knew what he was going to say. Part of her recognised the danger and part of her longed for him to say it.

But she was mistaken. 'Many other things,' Matt went on. 'The most important, perhaps, is getting to understand, however sketchily, how the Japanese mind works in business matters. Because until you know that it's next to impossible to make any useful contacts here.'

She let out her breath, fighting the need to burst

into stupid giggles. Of course, it was business that Matt was interested in. She occupied a very minuscule part of his attention. She drained her coffee mug and composed her face. 'You've been here before—do you feel that you understand Japanese businessmen?' That sounded like a reasonable question, she complimented herself. If she could keep the conversation on this level it would make things much easier.

'I believe I know a little about them, but only, perhaps, surface things. What I do know I respect. They're always polite and courteous and always scrupulously honest at every level of money transactions. They're very proud of their country, although they're trained to play down their own achievements—which are quite astounding in the economic line. They aren't afraid of hard work and they are intensely loyal to the company that employs them—generally for the whole of their working life. There are many things I admire about the Japanese—one of the most important being that loyalty.' Philippa had hardly followed what he had been saying. She had been watching his face as he spoke, noticing the little wrinkles at the corners of his eyes, the way his dark hair grew at his temples, his mouth——

'Don't you agree?' he asked.

She looked blank. 'Um?'

'Don't you agree that loyalty is a most important quality in a firm's employees?'

Her blue eyes opened very wide. 'Well, of course. It's obvious, isn't it?'

'Not to everyone it isn't, unfortunately.' He looked down at his plate as he spoke. Then, abruptly, he lifted his eyes to Philippa's. 'I believe that loyalty is the first essential in any company. Unless you can trust the people you work with you might as well give up, don't you think?'

She stared back at him. Why was he making such an issue of it?

The way he spoke, the way he was looking at her, told her that his words held a significance beyond their surface meaning. Was he trying to tell her something? He had almost accused her of spying on him. Was he trying to reassure her, perhaps to put her off the scent? But she felt that in some strange way they were crossing swords and she had to take the question as seriously as he had asked it. She had to keep her end up.

'Of course I do.' She met his narrowed gaze levelly. There was no difficulty in answering that question—her life had taught her all about what disloyalty can lead to on the personal level, and the business level could be just as important, though not so heartbreaking. 'I think disloyalty is utterly horrible,' she said vehemently. 'It should be one of the seven deadly sins.' She glanced round the busy, noisy coffee-shop, and pulled a wry face. 'Oh dear, we *are* getting into a deep discussion! This hardly seems the place.'

'No, you're right.' Matt was smiling again now. 'We'll discuss it some other time, along with the other deadly sins. Shall we go back to our rooms if you've finished and I'll show you what I want typing and leave you to it. I've got one or two calls to make.'

It took Philippa a little while to accustom herself to the electronic typewriter. She hadn't done any typing since business school, and then only the necessary work to pass her examinations. She hadn't admitted it to Matt, but after she qualified in her computer studies she had taken a six-months' secretarial course as well. 'Just in case,' Gran had told her. 'You can't have too many strings to your bow.'

Remembering that made Philippa think about Gran, and that reminded her again how completely alone she was. She had no idea where her father was, and her mother hardly bothered to keep in touch at all. Just a card for birthday and Christmas from South Africa, and that was all. Oh, why did Gran have to die? she thought, and suddenly her throat choked up. But she blinked away the tears resolutely and went on with the chore of deciphering Matt's scribbled notes. Self-pity was an indulgence she couldn't allow herself.

The work that he had set her took several hours to complete and by the time she had finished it was almost dark. She stood up and stretched stiffly to ease her aching muscles and went across to look out of the window. Far below, the lights had come on in the street and to her left she could see what looked like a park. To the right the colours reflected in the sky suggested that the centre of the city, with its blaze of neon signs, couldn't be far away. She felt a quirk of excitement and her spirits lifted. She would ask Matt, when he returned, if they could go out and see the Ginza. She had read of it as the most glittering and fascinating street in the East. Meanwhile she would have a shower and change and be ready for anything the evening might produce.

Standing in the shower, with the cool water beating on her body in the refreshing jets, Philippa began to feel all the previous thrill and excitement about this trip returning. She had looked forward to it so much and been so disappointed when she found that Matthew Vane was taking Adrian's place that she had allowed herself to get nervous and dispirited. But after all, she was here, in Japan, and that was the important thing. As she dried herself with a fleecy green towel and splashed herself liberally with her favourite body lotion she vowed that she was jolly well going to enjoy herself to the full. She wasn't going to allow the diminishing Matthew Vane to diminish her. After all, he was only a man. He couldn't eat her.

And he *hadn't* lied to her. Somehow that made an enormous difference. She was almost sure, now, that Adrian had been wrong, and that Matthew wasn't involved in any underhand business. When he talked about loyalty a few hours ago in the coffee-shop he had sounded as if the idea of loyalty meant a great deal to him. Perhaps, she thought, he had been let down by someone important in his life—just as she had. Ah well, she would never know him well enough to ask him.

Back in the bedroom she renewed her make-up and changed into one of her new dresses—a rather smart number in a pattern of navy and citrus-green with a loose polo collar and four buttons at the back. She was putting the finishing touches to her hair, coiling it up on to the top of her head, when she heard Matthew come in.

He walked straight into the bedroom and sank into a chair. 'Hey, don't you know it's bad manners to walk into a lady's bedroom without knocking?' Philippa asked the question to him through the mirror, without turning round.

She saw the grin pull at his mouth. 'Sorry, I'll try and remember. No harm done though, you're quite decent. Very decent indeed,' he added as she got to her feet. 'I like that dress—very snazzy. When I've recovered from a gruelling chase round Tokyo, trying to find an elusive office, I'll take you out and buy you a slap-up dinner. Meanwhile, be a good girl and find me a drink. Have a look on top of the fridge in the next room, there should be something there.'

'Certainly—sir.'

Philippa tripped across the bedroom, aware that his eyes were following her admiringly as the full skirt of her dress swished round her legs. Suddenly she felt light as air. There was a new friendliness about Matt that was reassuring and subtly exciting too. She hadn't felt this bubbling up of anticipation of an evening's outing since—well, for a very long time.

She returned with a small bottle and a glass. 'I'm not sure what this is,' she said doubtfully.

Matt examined the bottle with its Japanese characters on the label. 'Neither am I,' he admitted, 'but I'll risk it if you will. Bring another glass.'

Philippa went back and found a second glass, and Matt opened the bottle and poured some of the pale liquid out and sipped it. 'I'm still not sure what it is, but it tastes quite reasonable.' He lifted the glass. 'Here's to our co-operation and the success of our efforts.'

'Success,' echoed Philippa, and drank. 'It tastes like eau-de-cologne!'

'I don't drink much eau-de-cologne,' Matt said, straight-faced, and Philippa giggled. The evening was getting off to a good, light-hearted start.

'Now,' he said, 'I'm going to change, so unless you want to be entertained by a male strip-tease I suggest you remove yourself to the next room and wait for me there.'

He began to loosen his tie and Philippa, pulling a face at him, hurried out of the room and closed the door behind her.

She was standing looking down out of the window when he joined her, twenty minutes or so later. It was quite dark now and in the distance the coloured lights shone with an even brighter glow against the black velvet sky.

Matt came across and stood behind her. 'I've been wondering exactly where we are,' she said, her voice rising a tone or two because she was disturbingly conscious of the tall, male body close to her. 'I've read about the famous Ginza, where all the stores and restaurants and night-clubs are. I was just wondering if it was somewhere down there, where you can see the coloured lights in the sky.'

He put a hand round her shoulders and her toes curled up inside her sandals. 'Let's go and find out, shall we?' he said. 'Do you fancy eating?'

'Oh yes! I'm starving.' She turned her head, laughing, and their eyes met. His face was only inches away and he was looking at her oddly, the dark lashes lowered. 'I'm hungry too,' he said, slowly and deliberately. 'Only perhaps for a different kind of sustenance, just at the moment.'

Philippa swallowed. She wasn't sure that she knew how to handle this. She had thought, since Gerald, that she was an expert in coping with this kind of situation long before it got out of hand. But no man

as sexily magnetic as Matthew Vane had made a pass
at her. To wriggle out of his arms would be
intolerably gauche, but to stay where she was, with
both his hands on her shoulders and her face on a
level with his strong, bronzed throat, where he had
left his white shirt unbuttoned, was asking to be
kissed.

'I—I don't think——' she began huskily.

He chuckled. 'That's what I like to hear! Women
do too much thinking at times like this. Look at me,
Philippa.'

With some difficulty she lifted her head. His dark
hair was gleaming after his shower, his eyes were
smiling into hers, his lips were parted slightly over
strong, even teeth. She breathed in the clean,
masculine smell of him and her head spun.

When she felt his lips on hers it was as if she were
softening like wax beside a furnace. His mouth
brushed hers backwards and forwards teasingly,
then moved to her ear, following her hairline round
to the other ear and burying itself in the hollow of her
neck. She stood very still, feeling the slow-burning
fuse begin to ignite in her, feeling a pressure behind
her ribs as her breathing became jerky. For a
moment his left hand came up and closed softly
round her breast and she gave a short gasp. His
mouth found hers again, his tongue tracing the line
of her lips. She felt her own lips relaxing, parting.

When he put her away from him and held her at
arms' length, looking down into her face, she could
have wept because she wanted the blissful tension to
go on and on.

'Have you any idea,' he said slowly, 'how beautiful
you are, Philippa Marsden?'

She wasn't beautiful. She knew she wasn't. Attractive, perhaps, as hundreds of other girls are attractive. But beautiful—no! Not like that Heidi girl he had had with him at the hotel in Warwick.

She drew in a deep, steadying breath. Remembering the Heidi woman had brought her back to earth with a bump. 'Is that your usual line, Mr Vane?' she enquired. 'If so, isn't it a little crude, wouldn't you say?'

She saw the flash of anger in his steel-grey eyes and felt a squeeze of fear. 'What sort of a remark is that?' His voice was stony. 'I pay you a sincere compliment and you accuse me of being crude. Or was it my technique that didn't suit your taste?'

Oh lordy, now she had insulted him—she had touched him on the spot that hurts a man most, and certainly she hadn't intended to do that. For the first time she was conscious of the power that a girl has over a man and she wasn't sure that she wanted it.

'Oh, *please*.' She put her hand on his arm. 'That wasn't what I meant. I just meant that I know quite well I'm not beautiful that's all.'

'And you thought I was laying it on a little thick, in order to enhance my own chances of persuading you into my bed?'

'We-ell——' To her own amazement Philippa felt her mouth stretch into a small smile, and her eyes lift to his under long, silky lashes. 'I must admit the thought did occur to me.'

He burst into a roar of laughter. 'D'you know, I find I like you, Philippa. And that's a real compliment, one I don't often offer to a woman. So it wasn't my sexual technique you were complaining about?'

She laughed then. 'I wouldn't call myself an expert on these matters. I'm sure you're terrific. But as I don't intend to find out, the subject doesn't arise.'

Matt was standing quite still, surveying her oddly. 'Has anyone ever told you, Miss Marsden, that talking about love is making it?'

She raised clear blue eyes to his. 'Then hadn't we better go out and find a place to eat?' she said innocently.

He continued to look at her for a moment longer, speculative, thoughtful. Then suddenly he took her hand in his and drew her towards the door. 'Come along, Pippa,' he said with a wide grin. 'We'll go out and paint Tokyo red, white and blue!'

CHAPTER FIVE

'WE'LL eat "Western" this evening,' Matt announced as they made their way along the wide crowded streets, every few yards bringing them nearer to the blaze of neons that coloured the blackness above. 'You need time to get used to Japanese food and to eating with chopsticks.'

'Oh, but——' Philippa began. She wanted to tell him that she had bought a pair of chopsticks a fortnight ago and had been practising with them. At first it had proved frustrating, but eventually she had mastered the art. She was proud of the fact that she could even pick up a pea with the implements. But the noise around them drowned her words.

Matt took her hand and forged his way through the milling crowd, pulling her behind him like a speedboat towing a surfboard rider. The lights were all around them now, winking and flashing high up towards the sky in every colour of the rainbow. Philippa saw a board marked GINZA in huge letters. Now she knew she was really in Tokyo—the Tokyo she had read about, poring over her books from the library in bed at night. A modern city—self-confident, glittering, noisy, stunning. An atmosphere of success permeated the whole place.

Matt was in a hurry and Philippa had no choice but to follow him, although she would have loved to stop and stare into the brightly-lit windows of the huge department stores. She caught glimpses, as they cut their way through the crowd, of mink coats, of exotic high-fashion garments and sumptuous kimonos in silks and brocades, heavily encrusted with embroidery, of flowers and toys and pottery and jewellery and every kind of electronic marvel. The doors of bars and restaurants stood open and succulent cooking smells hung faintly in the air, together with the throb of pop music.

'This'll do.' Matt stopped before an imposing doorway and they were ushered inside the restaurant by a smiling, bowing, uniformed doorman. They were shown to a table in an alcove of bamboo screens where the noise of the street was muted to a distant murmur, the lighting subdued to a restful glow. The air was cool and smelled of flowers. It was the kind of place, Philippa recognised, where it cost a small fortune to eat a meal. But as she didn't have to pay for it she settled down to enjoy herself.

'This is lovely,' she said. 'Very relaxing.'

'That was the idea.' Matt studied the bill of fare as a waiter hovered attentively. 'It caters for Americans and is the best place in Tokyo to come for a grilled steak. Does that appeal to you?'

'Oh yes, please.' Philippa was ravenous. Excitement seemed to be having the effect of stimulating her appetite and everything about this evening seemed vastly exciting. Not least the man sitting opposite, smiling at her under long dark lashes with a smile that told her he was glad to be here with her. Even if he were only being polite it made her feel good. It was very odd how suddenly she had begun to like him. More than "like" perhaps—but she mustn't let herself get carried away by the man's charisma. It was enough that he was part of this whole wonderful experience that she had so looked forward to, and that it was all happening *now*.

She didn't know that her eyes were shining deeply blue, that her cheeks were glowing and her lips were softly parted over pretty, even white teeth. She only knew that she was enjoying herself.

The steaks were pink and succulent, served with exotic salad. 'American food,' Matt told her. 'They import beef specially for Westerners. There isn't much meat eaten by Japanese—fish is their speciality. But maybe we'll try that tomorrow.' He looked across the table at her. 'O.K., Philippa? Happy?'

'Yes, thank you,' she said, spearing a tender piece of steak. 'I'm quite ashamed of my appetite.'

'No need. Appetites—all kinds—are what makes the world function. Without appetites we should all die of hunger. And—to mention another kind of appetite—the population would decrease alarmingly.' The look he gave her under his long, dark lashes was quite explicit and made her cheeks go hot.

'I thought you said——' she began.

'——that talking about love is making it. I did. But it's the next best thing—and a fascinating subject for conversation, don't you think?'

'No,' said Philippa, with mock severity, 'I don't.' She might be standing at the gates of his world of sophistication, but she hadn't the confidence to go in yet. 'Let's talk about something else.'

'Why not?' he said easily. 'We have plenty of time.'

The way he was looking at her made her inside squeeze up and she didn't dare to enquire what he meant. Plenty of time for what? She thought she knew, and that 'plenty of time' was a respite, in which she had to gather enough strength to refuse what it was he expected of her.

'Now where?' asked Matt, when they came out into the crowded Ginza again. 'I suppose the sensible thing would be to go back to the hotel and get a good night's sleep, but as you're so keen to sample the Japanese way of life perhaps we might try a night-club first.'

By now Philippa was feeling so mellow that she was quite content to go where he led, and a few minutes later they were inside the scented cavernous dimness of her very first night-club. At first she could hardly see anything except the twirling, writhing bodies of the dancers who were performing a floor show. The colours of their costumes, under the spotlights, were so vivid that they hurt the eyes, and as Matt and Philippa made their way to a small side table, the dance rose to a final frenzy. The twanging music of a hidden band died away and the dancers left the floor. As the spotlights went out it was possible to see around the low room with its lanterns in all colours of the rainbow, thick festoons of greenery and plastic flowers. It was buzzing with talk, hazy with smoke, crammed with tables—most of them occupied.

A smiling hostess in a pink silk dress that left little to the imagination and with a pink rose in her hair brought them drinks. Matt, paying, grinned towards Philippa and murmured wryly, 'My expense account won't cover this sort of lark, I fear. We won't stay too long. This is just to further your education, my dear. Drink up.'

The band had started to play again, Western pop music now. Couples were drifting on to the small floor-space. Matt stood up. 'Come along, let's be devils,' he grinned, and held out his arms. The next moment Philippa found herself held close as they moved slowly round the floor, to the insistent slow beat of the music. More couples came on to the floor until it was impossible to make progress. But she was still held close against Matt's firm body as they swayed to the music. His cheek was resting against her hair and when she reached up and linked her arms round his neck it seemed the most natural thing in the world. She had stopped caring about giving him the wrong impression. She just wanted this moment to go on for ever, wanted to be in his arms, their two bodies pressed intimately together. She tipped back her head, her lips parted invitingly.

But the music stopped and Matt led her off the floor. 'I think,' he said, 'that we'd better go. If we stay on we'll be plied with more drink, and you've had enough already, Philippa.'

It was like a smack in the face. Hot with humiliation, she followed him out of the night-club, miserably regretting that she had lowered her guard, that she had let him know the effect he was having on her. Idiot! she berated herself as they made their way back to the hotel. Stupid fool, what did you think you were doing?

In the hotel lift she composed her face into a cool mask and kept as far away from Matt as was possible in the small space. As they reached the suite she yawned delicately.

'Thank you for a delightful meal,' she said politely. 'And now I'd like to have a long, long sleep, and be ready for work tomorrow.' If she ignored completely that moment of weakness in the night-club, perhaps she could pretend that it had never happened. Perhaps he hadn't noticed, she tried to convince herself.

But the narrow smile that he slid towards her quickly removed that frail comfort from her mind. 'Sleep? Is that really what you want, Pippa?' Spoken in his deep, drawling voice her pet name sounded like a physical caress.

She swallowed. 'Yes,' she said firmly. 'Sleep. And if you had anything else in mind, Mr Vane, please forget it.'

He was laughing at her again, the brute. It dented her self-confidence when he laughed at her. 'Forget it? You're asking the impossible, my girl. But first we must do our duty and see how Sam and Rex are getting along.' He sat down on the bed and lifted the telephone receiver, consulted his notebook, and dialled.

Philippa heard only one side of the conversation with Sam that followed. Matt's contribution amounted to, 'Yes. Yes. Yes—that's good. Yes, we're fine. Philippa's rather tired after the journey. Yes, we'll meet up tomorrow lunchtime, around midday. We'll come to your hotel, O.K?'

He replaced the receiver. 'They seem to have settled in. They're going along to this trade fair tomorrow morning. I'd like to have a look at it myself in the afternoon. Now, let's forget about business and make ourselves comfortable for the night. What do you drink before you go to bed, Philippa?'

'Tea,' she said promptly. 'Do you suppose there's any real tea here, or will it be that bright green variety that's served everywhere?'

'Let's see.' He began to poke about the wide shelf on which were arrayed the small fridge, a kettle, cups on a tray, and a variety of rather beautifully decorated containers. 'Home from home,' he mused, opening the lids. 'Coffee, biscuits, and—ah yes, tea bags. Real tea,' he added with a smile as he filled the kettle and switched it on.

Philippa went through to the bathroom. As she dried her hands she stared back at herself in the mirror. Huge blue eyes met hers doubtfully. What next? she wondered, and her heart began to beat uncomfortably against her ribs. She didn't intend to repeat her idiotic performance of a little while ago at the night-club, that was for sure. Face it, Philippa, you wanted him to kiss you. But he hadn't; instead he had hurried you away with a snide remark that you'd had enough to drink.

Now, how about that logic you learned at college? If Matt had wanted to start something, that would have been the time to do it. As he hadn't, the assumption was that he didn't want to—or at any rate that he didn't intend to. Very well reasoned, Philippa. Full marks. And if he didn't want to start anything, she certainly didn't, she told herself firmly.

It was easier to go back into the sitting-room after that. As they sat together on the divan drinking tea Matt talked about the programme for the next day. 'I've got a meeting in the morning, I won't need you there, so you can do some more typing for me. Then we'll join Sam and Rex and compare notes.'

'Couldn't I come to the meeting with you? I thought that was a personal secretary's job.' She had spent all afternoon typing out his notes—all technical stuff that hadn't meant a great deal to her—and the prospect of spending tomorrow morning at the same boring occupation wasn't exactly appealing. She hadn't come to Japan to sit in an anonymous hotel room typing notes that she was sure Matt could have had done when he got back to England.

'No,' he said, putting down his cup carefully, and not meeting her eyes, 'you can't come with me. The meeting is strictly confidential.'

'But I thought I was supposed to be a confidential secretary,' she argued. 'And anyway, you promised to explain what we're doing in Tokyo.'

He smiled at her suddenly, the dark smile that made her knees go weak. 'Did I really? But not at this time of night. You look tired, Pippa. And don't frown at me like that.'

His finger stroked the little vertical lines away from between her eyes, then passed upwards to smooth back her hair. His touch was feather-light and alarmingly erotic. 'Gorgeous hair,' he murmured. 'But I told you that before, didn't I?'

Somehow they were leaning back against the cushions and he had pulled her into his arms. 'Tired little Pippa,' he whispered. 'So soft and cuddly.' He drew her closer and his hand kneaded her breast very gently. Waves of shameless desire rippled through Philippa. It was no good trying to be logical; the man was dynamite and she might as well admit it. You couldn't apply logic to an electric generator, producing power by the millions of megawatts or whatever they produced. She sighed and let her head fall back on to his shoulder.

For a moment she felt his muscles tighten under the thin, smooth stuff of his shirt, as if he were warding off some hidden danger. Then he stood up and lifted her easily in his arms, carried her through to the bedroom and deposited her on the bed. 'Sleep for you, my pretty one.' He grinned down at her. 'That's an order.'

She stared up at him, blue eyes wide. Once again she had practically issued an invitation, and once again he had refused. So—she had been wrong about his intentions. He had no wish to lure her into his bed after all. She should be relieved, she supposed, but instead she felt as if a door had been slammed in her face.

But she mustn't at all costs show what she was feeling. She sat up on the bed. 'How will you manage on the divan? You'll need some blankets.' She tried to keep her tone practical and believed she had managed to control the shake in her voice.

'Don't worry, there are blankets under the cover, I looked. I suppose they reckon on having contingencies like this. Would you like to have the bathroom first? I'll go down to the bar and get myself a nightcap and leave you to it. Good night, Philippa. Sleep well.' He leant down and brushed her forehead with his lips. Then he went out of the suite and closed the door.

There were two loose cotton robes spread out on the bed and two pairs of slippers beneath it. Philippa transferred one set to the divan in the adjoining room. That would mark out the boundaries and remove any false impressions she might have given. Except that they weren't false, she admitted ruefully to herself. She had *wanted* to wrap her arm round

Matt's neck in the night-club; had *wanted* him to take her in his arms just now, when they sat on the divan. She had wanted to feel the touch of his hands on her with a hunger that shocked her. But that had been in the heat of the moment. Now, sanity had returned.

Slowly she undressed and put on the remaining cotton kimono. She brushed her teeth, washed her face, switched off the main room-light and climbed into the big bed. Then she adjusted the bedside lamp and settled down to read to the end of the thriller she had been reading on the plane. No way could she settle down to sleep until she was sure that Matt was safely tucked up in the next room. She still wasn't completely reassured that he didn't intend to share the bed with her. He was such a puzzling person. One minute he was gazing at her as if he would like to eat her, the next he had almost pushed her away. She couldn't believe that a man like Matt Vane would have too many finer feelings where his women were concerned. He was like Gerald in so many ways—not only in his looks; in his self-assurance, his urbane, relaxed personality. In the wicked glint of his eyes, the sexual challenge he exuded. And he had the same relentless streak in him, she recognised that already.

He was the kind of man that women fell in love with easily—and at their peril. She had fallen in love with Gerald without a struggle—and look where that had got her. No, she thought, not for me. Not again.

She heard him come in a few minutes later and an uneasy churning began inside her as she listened to the muffled sounds that came from the next room. He must be making up a bed on the divan now. A couple of thuds as he pulled off his shoes and dropped them on to the carpet. Then silence, and her imagination began to work overtime. He would be stripping off his clothes now—perhaps getting into the cotton kimono she had laid out for him. The one she was wearing was much too big for her slender body; she had had to pull it round her and turn up the sleeves. But its twin would fit Matt's large frame perfectly, she guessed. She heard the swish of the bathroom door sliding open, the muted rumble of the plumbing system.

Now he was back in the next room. Philippa found that her throat was aching with tension and she was holding her breath. Her eyes were fixed on the rim of light that came round the door. There was a click and the rim of light disappeared. She heard a soft thud and a long sigh.

She let out her breath and sank limply back against the pillow. Well, that was that. No night visitor for her, she could relax now and enjoy a good night's sleep. Resolutely she turned her eyes back to her book. She needed to lose herself in the story, to take her mind completely off all that had happened since the car drove away from Mrs Smithson's front door in Warwick.

Half an hour later, after she had read three pages over and over again and still hadn't the faintest idea what was happening in the plot, she closed the book, turned out the light and snuggled down to woo sleep.

She woke with a jolt to darkness and a feeling that something was terribly wrong. She put a hand to her head. She seemed to be swaying backwards and forwards, and she felt sick. She tried to remember what she had eaten at the restaurant that might have caused this—or was it the drink they had had at the night-club? Then, in the next room, there was a crash as some nameless object fell on to the floor. She put her hand out to the bedside lamp and pressed the switch. Nothing happened.

Suddenly she was swamped with fear. Her stomach was icy cold and her scalp prickled. 'Matt!' she croaked, and almost fell out of the bed and groped her way in the darkness to where the door ought to be.

The swaying was getting stronger now, but it wasn't inside her, it was outside; horribly, terrifyingly outside. The whole building—the whole gigantic skyscraper—was swaying like a tall tree in the wind. God, she thought—oh, my God, it's an earthquake! Shocking pictures of collapsed buildings in fogs of dust, of rescuers clawing at piles of rubble, of stretchers with their terrible covered burdens, reeled past her eyes in the blackness.

'Matt!' She tried again to call his name, but her mouth was as dry as sawdust.

Then she heard the door between them burst open and his arms were round her and he was holding her tightly against him, as great shudders racked her body. 'It's all right, Pippa. It's all right, love, I've got you safe. It'll be over in a minute. Look, the lights have come on again.'

The swaying had stopped. The bedside lamp was lit again. Philippa clung to Matt desperately, her fingers digging into his hair, as he picked her up and carried her across the room and laid her gently on the bed. 'That was a nasty one,' he said, 'but I've felt worse. These days all the new hotels are built to be earthquake-proof, you know. No real danger, but it's always alarming when you get a strong tremor like that. You'll find a notice about it in the next room. Tremors aren't too rare around these parts.'

'I didn't know——' she quavered, with a pathetic ghost of a smile. 'I only remembered we were on the twentieth floor. It seemed like a—' she gulped '—a long way down.'

He cuddled her against him as he lowered himself on to the bed beside her. 'Poor little Pippa, I should have remembered to warn you, you've had a bad shock. First a polar bear, then an earthquake, what's the next thing going to be?'

'And I thought I didn't scare easily,' she mourned. 'This trip was evidently designed to deflate my ego!'

She was getting back to normal by the second now. And it was so lovely being comforted by Matt, feeling his arms round her. Almost worth the moments of sheer terror.

'You're sure it's over?' She pressed closer to him and then—horrors!—she realised that he was naked. 'Oh! Oh, I'm sorry—I didn't know—I——' she gabbled wildly. She tried to move away, but his arm held her fast, the heat from his body reached her through the cotton kimono she was wearing.

He was laughing, and it was a good sound. It seemed to tell her, 'Nothing to be embarrassed about—we're friends, aren't we?'

Aloud he said, 'I don't go much for sleeping in these chic Japanese négligés myself, but I must admit you look very fetching in yours. Rather large, though, wouldn't you say?' He took hold of the front of the kimono and flapped it. Then his hand moved beneath it and touched her breast and she shivered deliciously.

'Oh, Pippa my sweet, what a very tempting morsel

you are,' he breathed huskily. His mouth brushed hers lightly, tempting, promising, questioning.

But somehow she managed to stay quiet in his arms, not pushing him away, not stiffening in defence, but not softening or yielding either. It was no good, she must *not* give him the encouragement he was waiting for. A tempting morsel, that was all she was to him, and he would swallow her up and then turn to the next tempting morsel—in the person of Heidi Jones, probably. It was no good. The chemistry between them was working potently, half drugging her senses, but she wasn't going to risk a repeat of the black misery that had followed the break-up with Gerald, and Matt was so like Gerald they might almost have been brothers. Love them and leave them, that was the way men like them functioned.

He took his mouth away and looked down at her. 'Pippa?' he breathed.

She shook her head, lips pressed together. 'No,' she said.

He drew in a ragged sigh and heaved himself off the bed. She watched his broad, strong back as he walked across the room. In the dim light from the bedside lamp his skin was golden, his waist narrow, his bottom firm and tense. The long, long legs with their fuzz of dark hair moved fluidly, like an athlete's legs. Oh, don't go, don't go, Philippa mourned, longing for him with an aching intensity. She couldn't bear him to go—if he went out now and closed the door between them she would run after him, she knew she would.

Matt disappeared into the next room and snapped on the light, but he didn't close the door, and a moment or two later he came back, pulling the cotton kimono round him. He pulled a basket chair up to the bed and sank into it, leaning back and looking steadily into her eyes.

'Why not?' he said, continuing the conversation as if there had been no break. 'It would take your mind off the fright you've just had in the most pleasant way possible.' When she said nothing he added, 'You're not a virgin, are you, Pippa?'

She looked away from him, across the dimly-lit room. 'Is that important?'

He shrugged. 'Not particularly. I just thought it might explain your reluctance, if you were.'

'Well, I'm not,' she snapped.

'Ah! The boy-friend would object? That eighth sin of disloyalty that you were talking about earlier?'

Philippa stuck her feet under the duvet and drew it up round her. 'Wrong on both counts,' she told him drily, and, for good measure, added, 'I suppose it wouldn't occur to you that I don't fancy you?'

'I think that would be a whopping big lie. We could set each other alight, and you know it. It happens like that sometimes—inexplicably, like the force of gravity.'

There was no possible answer to that one except to turn her head away so that she couldn't see him. 'I'm not prepared to discuss problems of physics with you at this time of night,' she said shortly.

'How right you are!' She could almost see the ironic smile although she wasn't looking at him. 'Well, let's discuss something else. I've no intention of leaving you on your own just yet in case we get another tremor.'

Her head shot round then. 'Oh, do you think——?'

'Probably not,' he said soothingly, 'but it's as well to stay awake for a time, just in case. So—if you're not willing to fall in with my suggestion about how we should pass the time, how about telling me your life story? That ought to take your mind off earthquakes.'

She wasn't sure she was ready to lower her guard with him. 'I thought you'd already looked me up in the files.'

'Oh, but that was only the facts. I know you're twenty-one. I know where you were educated, what exams you've passed. I know your hobbies are put down as music and reading. You've already told me you favour whodunnits for your spare-time reading. What about music?'

They seemed to be on fairly safe ground here. 'All sorts,' she said. 'Classical, Country and Western, jazz, pop when I feel like it. It depends on my mood.'

They discussed music for a time, amicably. Then, quite suddenly, Matt asked, 'And what sort of music does Adrian Banks go for?'

Philippa blinked. 'Well, I—I don't know.'

He raised dark brows. 'Really? Romantic evenings in his hotel room—and you don't know his taste in music? I thought music was part of every good seduction scene, like champagne and shaded lights.'

'You're the expert, as I said before,' Philippa snapped.

There was a long silence. Matt studied her face thoughtfully and she stared back at him. She would *not* give him the satisfaction of making her drop her eyes. The silence went on and on and tension built up in her until she was ready to scream.

Then he said quietly, 'So Adrian Banks isn't the

one. He isn't your lover?'

'You asked me that before, remember?' she re-
torted. 'Why do you keep on about Adrian and me?
We're just good friends, as the saying goes.'

'But you'd planned to share a room with him when
you got here, to Tokyo, hadn't you?'

'No.' She hesitated, because the thought *had*
occurred to her. 'Well, not exactly planned,' she
added honestly. 'I just thought——'

Oh lord, she was in such a muddle. This—this
inquisition, coming on top of her scare of a few
minutes ago, had left her mind numb. 'Don't *pester*
me like this,' she said crossly. 'Why are you so
interested in what Adrian is to me? Is it so important
to you?'

'As a matter of fact it is,' he said, and there was an
odd, serious note in his voice.

'I simply can't imagine why,' Philippa shrugged.
'But if you'd like to know the whole completely
uninteresting story, I'll tell you. Just over a fortnight
ago Adrian asked me to call in at his office. Until then
I'd never actually spoken to him since he came to
work at the branch. He said he was organising a
four-person team to come to Tokyo on a fact-finding
mission. He asked me if I'd like to join it and I said
yes. Since then I've had dinner with him twice and
we've discussed the trip. On each occasion he drove
me home to my digs and left me at the front door.
The other evening, after you told us that he wouldn't
be leading the team after all, I was disappointed and
surprised. I decided to call in at his hotel on the way
home and see him. He told me he too was disappointed but was quite in the dark as to the reason. He was
just leaving for his train and he offered to share his

taxi with me. As we came down the stairs you came into the hotel with—you came into the hotel and we met. And that, Mr Vane, is the sum total of my relationship with Adrian Banks, as it seems of such interest to you.'

Her mouth firmed and her eyes flashed dark blue. 'And now are you satisfied and will you shut up about it, because I'm very, very tired of being grilled on the subject!'

To her annoyance he was smiling. 'Very neatly expounded. You have quite a gift for self-expression, Pippa. Your training in computer programming would include a course in elementary logic, so I suppose that figures.'

Patronising beast! she thought angrily, but she restrained her urge to snap back at him. She didn't feel like starting a quarrel.

Matt was silent, leaning back in his chair, his eyes on the ceiling. Then once more he took her breath away as he lowered his head and shot at her, 'Well, if Adrian Banks isn't your lover, who is? Who's the lucky man who commands such loyalty from you?'

It was suddenly all too much. She was tired and still suffering from the after-effects of the shock she had had when the room began to sway like a storm-tossed boat under her feet. She couldn't take any more.

She wriggled down in the bed and buried her head in the pillow. 'Oh, go away,' she said in a muffled voice, and weak tears flooded into her eyes.

She heard the basket chair creak as he got out of it, felt his arms round her, his hand on her cheek, turning her head towards him. 'I'm sorry, Pippa, I'm an insensitive brute. Please don't cry. Have you got a hanky, there aren't any pockets in this fancy garment.'

'Tissues,' she gulped. 'There, on the table.'

He reached out to the bedside fitment and pulled a tissue from its box and put it in her hand. She dabbed her eyes and blew her nose and crumpled the tissue into a damp ball. He took it from her and dropped it in the waste-basket. 'Now,' he said, settling his long legs on the top of the bed covers and holding her in the circle of his arm, and pulling her head against his shoulder, 'let's make ourselves comfortable. And don't tell me to go away, because I haven't any intention of going. I doubt if there's any danger, but I'm certainly not going to leave you alone tonight.'

'Oh,' said Philippa in a very small voice. She had made a feeble stand against him and she couldn't do any more.

'And don't worry,' he said practically. 'I have reasonable control over myself, but if I find I can't sleep I can always get up and take a cold shower.'

She giggled weakly. 'What a ghastly thought—I hope it doesn't come to that.'

'I hope so too. Now, settle down and go to sleep, my dear.'

Suddenly she was stupid with tiredness. She felt like a clockwork toy that slows, stops and topples over as the spring relaxes. She yawned, closed her eyes and nestled like a kitten against Matt's broad chest with a blissful feeling of contentment.

She was drifting—drifting—— 'There isn't—isn't—any——' The words slurred. There was something she had to tell him, but she had forgotten what it was.

Philippa sank into the deepest sleep of her whole life.

CHAPTER SIX

'PHILIPPA!'

Her name sounded through cotton-wool layers of sleep. She opened her eyes a slit, wincing as bright shafts of sunlight struck them through the window where the curtains had been drawn back.

'Philippa, are you awake?' The bedroom door opened and then someone was standing beside the bed, someone tall and broad and male. Definitely *not* Mrs Smithson reminding her that breakfast was on the table. She opened her eyes wider.

'You *have* had a good long sleep, haven't you?' said Matthew. 'But I'm afraid it's wakey-wakey time now.'

The deep, ironic voice, the unexpectedly playful words, had her awake immediately. Memory came rushing back like a tide rolling on to the shore, one wave tossing over the one before it. Philippa dragged herself up in the bed, clutching the cotton robe round her.

She blinked up at the man standing beside the bed, immaculate in his charcoal suit, pale blue shirt and navy tie, dark hair neatly brushed, firm chin smoothly shaven. The perfect picture of the top executive, groomed and ready for the day's important business. She was his secretary and here she was, lolling in bed. She rubbed her eyes. God, she felt awful!

'Sorry,' she mumbled. 'Just give me five minutes.'

He grinned sceptically. 'Five minutes? I'll believe

114

it when I see it. Breakfast's on next door. I'll get on with mine, I've got an early appointment.' But he still stood looking down at her in the big bed, her cheeks pink with sleep. Then he leaned over and rumpled her coppery curls. 'Sleepy puss,' he said, and went out of the room.

Philippa slid out of bed. The cover on the opposite side had been straightened, but the pillow still bore the indentation of a head that wasn't hers. 'I'm not going to leave you on your own tonight,' he had said. Had he stayed on top of the covers or had he pushed them back and slipped in beside her? Close—so close, their limbs touching.

Philippa's heart flipped and a slow heat began to rise through her body. She staggered across the room and turned on the shower.

Matt looked up from the table when she went into the sitting-room and consulted his watch. 'Seven minutes. Not bad,' he said. 'Coffee?' He poured a cup from a reddish round pot, so beautifully decorated that it might have come off a museum shelf.

'Thank you.' Philippa sat down opposite and gulped the coffee, which was almost cold by now, but fairly strong and definitely refreshing. She crumbled a roll. 'I really am sorry for being such a pain last night. It won't happen again. Polar bears, earthquakes, anything else that comes along—I promise to keep my cool in future.'

He regarded her quizzically. 'Don't make rash promises—you never know what might happen.' He pushed back his chair and stood up. 'Now I must be getting along, I have an appointment at nine-thirty and it's very unwise to keep a Japanese businessman waiting. They're extremely polite and courteous themselves and great on punctuality.'

Philippa put her cup down. 'Please, couldn't I come with you? I know you said you wouldn't need me, but there must be something I could do to help. Take some notes perhaps? I don't write shorthand, but——'

'No,' he snapped. 'There's nothing you could do. You just stay here and get on with the typing.'

She turned her head away, biting her lip. She wasn't going to cry again, was she? No, no, *no*, she wasn't.

'Philippa,' he said in an odd tone. 'Just why are you so keen to come with me?' He didn't sound irritated now, he sounded curious, almost worried.

'Because—because——' She spread out her hands, searching for the right words. 'Because when I'm alone here I seem to shrink into nothing. I don't exist any longer. I suppose it's because Tokyo's such a vast place and I—I don't know where you are, and there's—there's nobody. If you could just tell me the name of the company you're going to see, or the telephone number, I could——'

He heaved a sigh of resignation. 'O.K., then, I suppose you'd better come along with me. Hurry, though.'

'Oh, thank you!' She scuttled back into the bedroom and pulled her suit jacket from its hanger. She smoothed down the silver-grey skirt over her hips and adjusted the collar of her navy crêpe blouse. She picked up her handbag and leant down to take a quick look at herself in the mirror on the dressing-table and found she was smiling. She had to admit to herself, now, that she had been less than honest in what she had said to Matt. What she needed more than anything was some proof that he was conducting straightforward business. The hint of secrecy alarmed and confused her. It had seemed to her that he was deliberately keeping her out of anything that touched on business matters. But now he was taking her along with him so she must have got the wrong impression. It was a great relief.

'I'm ready,' she said, running back into the sitting-room.

Matt was standing by the door, waiting. His dark eyes travelled over her as she approached him, slowly, appreciatively. 'Very nice too,' he said. 'What a pity there are all these meetings to get through. But tonight we'll do something exciting. I promise you. Now come along, let's try our luck with a taxi.' He put his arm casually round her as they walked along the corridor to the lift and Philippa had to brace herself to walk straight and not lean against him. Damn the man, why did he have to be so fatally sexy? It complicated everything. And what was it he had in mind for tonight that was 'exciting'? The heat began crawling up her body again and she kept as far away from him as she could in the lift.

Outside the hotel Tokyo burst into teeming, roaring life. Philippa had never seen anything like it, not in the Birmingham rush-hour, not even on her rare visits to London. Traffic was solid in the street, moving at a snail's pace. Overpasses snaked over the streets, making bewildering patterns against the high buildings. The pavements were solidly packed with people. Matt spoke to the hotel doorman and within minutes a taxi appeared as if by magic. The door opened by remote control and Philippa climbed in beside Matt, who handed the driver a paper with

Japanese characters on it.

'Few of the taxi-drivers speak English,' Matt explained. 'You need to have your destination written down or you find yourself in a hell of a mess—as I've done more than once.'

Philippa couldn't imagine a situation that Matt couldn't cope with, but she just smiled towards the driver's back and said, 'He's terribly smart, though. A taxi-driver wearing white gloves! And the taxi's so spotless and polished. Makes you feel like royalty.'

'I imagine that's the idea,' said Matt drily. 'Tokyo's probably the cleanest city in the world, as well as being the second largest. The Japanese are rightly proud of it. Some day,' he added, looking out of the window at the immovable cars that surrounded them, 'they may get down to doing something about their traffic problem. Ah, here we go now,' as the block started to break up.

After innumerable stops and starts they were in a street lined with high modern buildings, squeezed tightly together as if every inch of space were valuable—which it probably was. 'The Maranouchi district,' Matt told her. 'Most of the head offices of banks, shipping and insurance are here, as well as big business. The architecture is fairly undistinguished. Disappointed?'

His ironic tone again. Philippa raised her chin. 'Why should I be? I've read about Tokyo, I didn't expect it to be all cherry blossom and mist-wreathed mountains and peaceful streams, you know.'

He grinned. 'The puss has claws!' He put a hand on her knee and kept it there. 'Sorry, Pippa, I mustn't tease you.'

She looked down at his hand; it seemed to be

burning a hole through her thin silver-grey skirt and she removed her own hand, looking away.

The office that Matt was visiting was in one of the tallest buildings, with an impressively large foyer. They were whisked up in a lift by a smiling porter and bowed into a luxurious suite of rooms. A tiny, pretty secretary in a smart dress took Matt's card and indicated that they should sit in one of the deep leather lounge-seats in what appeared to be a waiting-room. 'You like tea—coffee?'

'Thank you—tea,' Matt nodded, and the smiling girl departed with a deep bow. He chuckled. 'Our office staff could learn something about service from these people!'

A tray was set before them by yet another smartly-dressed girl. The tea was in small handle-less bowls and was bright green in colour. Philippa regarded it dubiously. 'Try it,' Matt laughed at her expression. 'It's an acquired taste, but if you're going to get the feel of Japan—which you seem so keen on—green tea is a "must".'

The first young secretary appeared again. 'Mr Kiwada will see you now, Mr Fane,' she trilled in her high, soft voice. 'Please to follow me.'

Philippa got to her feet when Matt did, but he gestured to her to sit down again. 'You can wait here and learn to like green tea,' he said with a smile.

He must have seen the way her face dropped, for he added rather curtly, 'I don't want you with me on this meeting, is that understood?'

He followed the secretary out of the room, leaving Philippa with two bowls of green tea and an uncomfortable feeling that he was quite deliberately keeping her ignorant of everything that was going on here.

The meeting went on and on. Philippa drank both bowls of tea and tried to persuade herself that she was getting a taste for the stuff. There were shiny colour magazines on the table, in both Japanese and English, but after a quick glance at the pictures she put them down. She didn't feel like reading. Instead she gazed through the glass partition at the far end of the room into a vast, open-plan office with computer stations dotted about at intervals, divided by screens and great tubs of flowering plants. Hardly any sound reached her through the glass and the clerks in the office seemed to be part of some vision of the future as they bent over their desks or moved noiselessly around. She recalled the small, stacked office where she worked back in England with Sam and Rex and felt almost homesick. This trip was turning out so totally different from anything she had expected and hoped for.

And why was Matt so keen to keep her out of any business that he was transacting here? That was the question that nagged at her on and off—although she had to admit that most of the time they were together she forgot all about it.

But it returned with a nasty jolt when finally she saw his tall figure approaching across the office beyond the glass partition. He was talking to the much shorter Japanese man walking beside him, who was smiling and nodding. You never could tell, of course, but the two of them gave the immediate impression of having concluded a business deal to the greatest satisfaction of everyone concerned.

Well, fine, thought Philippa. Or it would have

been fine if she hadn't been almost sure that the man walking beside Matt was the same one who had been sitting across the table from him in the corner of the lounge yesterday, when they had seemed to her as if they might be—be plotting something. Or was she letting her imagination run away with her?

'Ah, here you still are, Philippa.' Matt sounded affable as he introduced her to Mr Kiwada as his valued personal secretary (that was a laugh, Philippa thought grimly) and there was a good deal of smiling and bowing and compliments, and then they were going down in the lift and finally reaching the busy street again.

Matt consulted his watch. 'We may as well make our way to Sam's hotel. If they're not in yet we can wait,' he said, summoning a passing taxi.

This time it was a longer ride. Matt was silent and seemed preoccupied, and Philippa stared out of the window as the taxi wove its way in the stop-start manner she was getting accustomed to through the noise of the densely packed traffic. She would be glad to meet Sam and Rex; it would make things seem more ordinary. Perhaps she could find out from Sam some details of why they were all here in Tokyo.

Half an hour later the four of them were sitting in the lounge-bar of Sam's hotel, which was obviously a far more modest one than the palatial affair where Matt and Philippa were staying. She wondered uneasily again why Adrian had made such a point of separating the two halves of his team when he did the booking.

'Cheers, what's the news from your front?' Matt lifted his glass of beer towards Sam and Rex.

'Everything okey-doke.' Sam smiled his usual laconic smile, but Philippa noticed how he glanced at Rex in a guarded sort of way. 'The show here has to be seen to be believed. Acres of it! Bigger than the N.E.C. in Birmingham.'

The talk became technical. Sam was full of enthusiasm for many of the exhibits. 'They can teach us a thing or two, but in some things I'd say we have the edge at present. Take modems——'

They took modems while they quaffed two more glasses of Sapporo beer, which seemed to be Japan's favourite. Rex was apparently listening but hardly joined in the conversation, his small eyes darting backwards and forwards between the other two men, while he chain-smoked cigarettes until Sam stopped him with a nudge and a 'Hey, steady on, chum, ladies present!'

Philippa did her best to follow the talk, but Matt and Sam were exploring the higher reaches of computer language which finally left her behind. She contented herself with sipping her beer and watching Matt's face as he talked. His eyes lit with enthusiasm, he gestured with his hands as he argued, put forward a new point. All the irony that he turned on *her* was gone, he was a hundred per cent the dedicated professional, immersed in his own subject. She found herself fascinated by him in an entirely new way—nothing to do with sex. Well, hardly anything. This was sheer admiration for someone who was a super-expert in her own, much humbler, sphere.

Oh no, Adrian, you're wrong, she found herself deciding. This man wasn't—couldn't possibly be—a cheat and a fraud. She wasn't going to let herself harbour another suspicious thought about him. He was wonderful, marvellous, a super-star. Her eyes were dreamy as she watched him.

Then something very odd happened. The poky, smoke-filled crowded bar suddenly changed. Everything became very clear and distinct. The dress of the Japanese girl behind the bar blossomed into gorgeous flower colours, the glasses glittered and shone in the shaft of sunlight that filtered through the small windows. The men sitting round the bar in their dark business suits, their black hair plastered down neatly, were all her greatest friends. Dazed, she turned back to Matt, and it was as if he knew. He broke off what he was saying and their eyes met and held in a long look. Philippa's inside began a slow sensuous churning that was almost painful. She put a hand to her throat. I'm in love, she thought very clearly, and a little smile touched her lips.

The rest of the afternoon passed in a dream. It was a wonderful exhibition, she supposed, because everyone was saying so as she trailed round the enormous area with the three men. The whole place was teeming with people; the noise was deafening, with the constant high-pitched conversation, the chatter of tannoys and the twanging of Japanese music in the background. But it was all like fairyland to Philippa, and even the stands showing heavy machinery had a quality of magic.

Once Matt turned to her and touched her hand. 'Good, don't you think?' He seemed to be including her deliberately, not wanting her to feel left out. And she smiled dazedly into the dark eyes that looked into hers and murmured, 'Oh yes—super,' and a little smile passed between them that had nothing to do with high-tech, or machinery, or anything else but their two selves. At least that was how it seemed to Philippa.

At some point in the afternoon they all stood at the bar eating hot-dogs and drinking more beer. Later they met two American men that Sam and Rex had palled up with. Philippa was vaguely conscious that the Americans were being very attentive to her and asking her questions about her job and eyeing her with interest, but nothing really registered with her except Matt. Matt. Matt. Matt. His name kept going round and round her head.

When, at last, Sam groaned that his feet had had it for the day, the three of them left the exhibition hall and sat on a low wall outside, overlooking an artificial lake. Rex had left them some time ago, pleading a headache, and returned to the hotel.

Sam shook his head. 'Old Rex isn't too happy—worried about his mum. She's in a nursing-home in Leamington.'

Matt frowned. 'That's bad. Tell him to phone through and enquire—it can go on the hotel bill,' he said, and Sam promised to do that.

He's kind, Philippa thought, her eyes going to Matt's face; he really cares about Rex's problem. She could find nothing but good about him now.

He was consulting his watch. 'I've got plans to give Philippa a taste of the other Japan this evening. I've got seats for the theatre—the Kabuki Theatre. I didn't suppose you and Rex would have been keen. Would you?'

Sam grimaced and his monkey face looked even more monkeyish. 'No, ta very much. I'm not so hot on culture. We're joining those American blokes for a long session at a pin-ball parlour. What do they call is—*pachinko*. Have you seen these places? Hundreds and hundreds of machines in rows, all clacking away like mad. Some of the old folk spend all day there—they take their lunch in paper bags. Well, I'll love you and leave you. Tomorrow we're booked to go to the Yamaga factory.'

'Fine,' said Matt heartily. 'I wish I could come with you, but I've got two meetings fixed for tomorrow. But the factory will fill in your last day. We'll be in touch.' He turned to Philippa. 'Hang on here a bit while I see if I can nab a taxi.'

Philippa stood beside Sam, watching Matt's broad back disappearing into the crowd around the exhibition hall. 'Well, love, enjoying the trip?' Sam turned his round glasses benevolently upon her.

'Oh yes, it's fascinating. Tokyo just knocks you on the head, doesn't it?' She had to raise her voice to be heard above the roar of the traffic, trying to sound ordinary, as if she hadn't just been knocked on the head by a discovery that had nothing to do with Tokyo.

'Good,' said Sam. 'And how are you getting on with our esteemed boss?'

'Oh, fine. Fine.' Now her voice did really sound false, even above the traffice, and she saw Sam looking rather hard at her, but he didn't say any more, and at that moment Matt shouted and waved and she took a hurried leave of Sam and fell into the taxi that was waiting.

'We should really have taken the subway,' said Matt, 'that would have extended your knowledge of Tokyo no end. But we're getting dangerously near the rush-hour and I wouldn't subject you to that, my sweet child. Sardines aren't in it at the rush-hour! The guards actually push people in until the carriages are bulging. Rather like pushing the last couple of shirts into a washing-machine.'

Philippa laughed. Sitting close to Matt, so close that their thighs were only inches apart, was making her feel lightheaded. 'What do you know about packing washing-machines, Mr Vane?'

'Oh, you'd be surprised. I've got all mod cons in my flat at the top of the Manor. I'll show you when we get back. I've got plans to put Henry in charge of all the electrics in the flat.'

'Henry?'

'Henry is my personal computer—the latest one. I got my first one when I was quite a lad and my mother christened it Henry. My mother, as you may have guessed, is of a whimsical turn of mind, bless her.' His mouth curved into an affectionate smile. 'Some years, and even more computers later, each new one is still Henry. I think the present one is Henry Mark Fourteen.'

Philippa tried to imagine Matt sitting up in his flat with Henry. It was very much more appealing than imagining him there with that Heidi woman.

Suddenly she wanted to know all about him. It seemed ridiculous that she didn't know anything, really. 'And what does Henry Mark Fourteen do?'

'Very little, except look after my bank account at the moment. I'd like him to take over the lighting— you know, switch things on and off and all that, but I never seem to have time to do the programming.' He turned his head and looked at her. 'Perhaps you'd like to come up and help me tackle it some time? I've got as far as identifying the module numbers where I propose to link up direct output lines to the electrical equipment, but that's about all. Will you?'

'I'd love to—that would be fun.' Matt's flat in the evening, up at the top of the Manor. All the staff gone. The doors shut and the spotlights turned on to a working table. Mugs of coffee beside them. Their two heads close together, as they worked on something that interested them both. Just as hopeful as violins and roses, really. She chuckled and then turned it into a cough.

'We'll fix it up when we get back,' he said shortly, and then he didn't say any more, just looked out of the window as if he were thinking of something else. Would he remember that he'd asked her? Philippa wondered anxiously. Or was he already sorry he had?

She decided to change the subject. 'Did you really mean what you said about going to the Kabuki Theatre this evening?'

'If that's what you'd like. Would you?' Matt took her hand and turned it over and examined the palm with interest.

'Oh yes, I'd be thrilled to see it. Thank you.'

He was looking at her in a new kind of way. 'Thank *you*,' he said quietly, and kept her hand in his until they got back to the hotel.

Up in the suite Matt dragged off his tie with a groan of relief and unfastened the top button of his shirt. 'Something more informal is in order for this evening, I think,' he said. 'Dressing the part of the visiting executive can get somewhat tedious. Do you want the shower first or may I?' His eyes twinkled suddenly. 'Or how about sharing it?'

'Not funny.' Philippa's voice seemed to come from a long way away. She couldn't meet his look;

her eyes were fixed with fascination on the brown expanse of chest that was now exposed, a seam of crisp black hair running up the centre. Was this his way of starting an evening of flirtation—of innuendo, that could have only one end to it? She had to make up her mind here and now how she was going to react.

There wasn't any choice really. It would be asking for heartache to let herself start an affair with Matt that would last—how long? A couple of days at most. Tonight and tomorrow night, and then, next day, they would fly back to England and revert to their previous roles. He the big boss, the director of the branch; she the junior computer operator.

But what about his suggestion that she should help him with programming his personal computer—after office hours, of course? That would no doubt be fixed for evenings when Heidi (or one of his other women, because she was sure he must have others) wasn't available. She would take her place in the queue.

No, she told herself violently. Not again. I'll allow myself a little fantasy of being in love while we're here, but no further than that. Like being a teenager again and having a crush on some current heart-throb.

She walked past him into the bedroom, pulling off the jacket of her silver-grey suit. 'You have the shower first if you like. I've got to decide what to wear.' She managed a fairly convincing little laugh. 'It's going to be awfully difficult—I've got just two dresses with me.' That, she thought, would be the attitude that would see her through the evening. Light and jokey. Nothing serious.

Matt came up behind her and slid open the door of the closet where her two dresses hung, together with his own clothes—separated by a width of rail in the middle. 'Put this one on, it suits you.' He touched the full-skirted cotton dress in navy and citrus that she had worn yesterday. 'It makes your waist look even smaller. You've got a very tempting waist, my girl.' He said it almost as if he resented the fact. 'Look, I can almost span it with my two hands.'

She felt his hands on her, at the junction of her skirt and top, and caught her breath. She could feel herself swaying towards him and checked the movement just in time, turning it into an evasion, sliding out of his grasp with a light laugh. 'Wht is this—a session in a slimming club? Am I being measured for a personal diet?'

Matt didn't laugh. He leaned against the door of the closet, looking oddly uncertain of himself. 'I don't seem able to keep my hands off you,' he said in a puzzled voice. 'What are we going to do about it?'

'You mean what are *you* going to do about it?' Philippa refused to consider the question seriously.

He shook his head. 'Oh no, Pippa, it's not all me. You like me to touch you, don't you? Don't you?'

Suddenly the atmosphere in the bedroom changed, as if an electric charge had been released into it. Philippa found herself unable to move as he reached out and pulled her towards him, his hands on her shoulderblades. 'Don't you?' he whispered huskily. And then, 'Oh God, I want you so much,' as his mouth took hers, his hands slipping down to her hips to hold her against the revealing hardness of his body.

She shuddered violently, unable to resist the grip

of desire deep inside her that was almost pain. Her mouth moved against his, her fingers tangled in his warm, springy hair. Never in her life before had she felt such a surge of pure sexual need that was like liquid fire pouring through her. She knew dimly that she was powerless to resist anything that he cared to do with her now.

Matt lifted her in his arms and carried her to a big easy chair and held her on his knees, close against him, one arm round her thighs, the other pressing her soft breasts against him with a kind of desperation, his mouth buried in the curve of her neck. Her cheeks were against the crispness of his hair; she could smell the cologne he used on it, together with the clean smell of newly-washed hair. She was conscious of a pulse beating strongly somewhere— was it his, or hers, or a blending of the two? 'Darling——' he muttered. 'Oh, darling——'

Then, with a gusty intake of breath, he pushed her away and stood up, and she collapsed back into the chair, shivering. He didn't say a word, simply left her there and strode across the room. A moment later, through the haze of misery, she heard the shower being turned on. She laid her forehead weakly against the velvet back of the chair, waiting to get control of herself, her mind blank, only her body functioning without her consent.

Why? she asked herself helplessly. What was the game Matt was playing? Why hadn't he taken her then—when she had been so obviously, so humiliatingly willing? She felt as if the whole of her body were suffused with a painful blush. Slowly she got up from the chair and took down the navy and citrus dress from the closet and laid it on the bed, her

movements awkward and clumsy. What next—
would they be going to the theatre, as planned, or
had everything changed? She felt almost as disorient-
ated as she had done last night when the room had
swayed under her. Love was like an earthquake, it
struck suddenly, putting you off balance, making
everything unreal and threatening.

Love? But it wasn't love she felt for Matt, it
couldn't be. You couldn't love anyone in just two
days. That feeling that had struck her in the bar,
when Sam and Rex were there, was just a romantic
fantasy, born out of the excitement of being in
Tokyo—that restless, dazzling, overwhelming city.
No, it wasn't love, it was just a strong sexual
attraction for a very sexy man, and that was
something she could deal with, surely? She should be
reassured, anyway. He had shown quite plainly that
although he wanted her he didn't intend to give in to
that weakness. She wondered if he had guilty
feelings about letting the Heidi girl down.
Somehow that didn't seem likely.

She bit her lip hard. She would never understand
Matt Vane, so what was the use of trying? But one
thing that she had learned in the last few minutes—
she was in danger of getting in far deeper with Matt
than she intended to. Next time he might not decide
to hold off, and she had to be prepared to resist both
him and herself. If she let Matt make love to her he
would spoil her for any other man for years—
perhaps for ever.

He came back into the bedroom, a green towel
knotted round his waist, his body gleaming after his
shower, his black hair standing in wet spikes. 'That's
better,' he grinned. 'Nothing like a cold shower, as I

remarked last night.' He slid her a sideways glance as he went over to the dressing-chest and pulled open a drawer. 'Sorry about all that, Philippa, it wasn't really on the agenda.'

'Just a passing temptation, was it?' she said lightly. 'Like happening to notice an open packet of chocolate mints lying around?'

He took out a silky cream shirt, his back to her. 'No,' he said. 'Not like that at all.' He turned and looked at her with brooding dark eyes. 'You know what's happening to us, don't you, Pippa? If I'd got you on the bed then, I couldn't have stopped. And that wasn't how I'd planned things. And I don't think you wanted it like that either, did you?'

'No,' she said slowly, 'I didn't want it like that.' Not just a quick release of passion, meaning nothing, leading nowhere.

He put down the shirt and turned, leaning against the chest, arms folded.

'Just what *do* you want out of life, Pippa? You're old enough to know. A career? Money? Power? Sex? Home and babies?' Somehow he managed to make the final three words faintly mocking.

'Assessing me for a job, Mr Vane?' she enquired flippantly. 'Send me a questionnaire and I might fill in the answers for you. And now, perhaps, you'll be good enough to take what you want from the bedroom and remove yourself before I'm ready to dress.' And with a swish of a silver skirt and a toss of coppery curls she repaired to the shower-room and slid the door closed with a firm click.

When she returned to the bedroom Matt was nowhere to be seen. She peeped through the open door and he wasn't in the sitting-room either. She

dressed quickly, refusing to let herself dwell on
what had just happened. She had to accept the fact
that Matt was behaving rather strangely, and that
was that. She wasn't likely to understand the man,
so it was no good trying to use her logical training to
sort out his actions or his intentions. She zipped
herself into the little navy and citrus dress and sat
down to apply rather more make-up to her face than
usual. Stroking mascara liberally on to her long
lashes and applying a poppy-red gloss to her lips
made her feel more confident, more sophisticated,
more capable of dealing with an enigma like Mr
Matt Vane.

She heard him come into the next room jut as she
put the final touch to her hair, which she had piled
up on top of her head, leaving a few wisps over her
ears. His head appeared round the bedroom door.
'Permission to enter?' he asked cautiously.

It was all right. He had put that strange little
scene behind him as she was trying to do. 'Certainly,
I'm all ready.'

He came into the room, surveying her with
pleasure. 'Very fetching, Miss Marsden. Please
accept this as a small token of my esteem.' He held
out an orchid, its golden curled petals streaked with
a green almost the same colour as the green on her
dress.

'Oh!' gasped Philippa. 'It's beautiful—exquisite!
Oh, thank you.' She held the lovely flower tenderly,
smiling. 'Nobody ever gave me an orchid before.'

Matt looked very bland. 'There's a first time for
everything, they tell me. Will you wear it?' He kept
a distance, not offering to pin it on for her. Flir-
tations were evidently out for the moment.

Philippa fastened the orchid to her collar. 'There, you matched the colour perfectly. Aren't you the clever one?'

His dark eyes were unreadable as they met hers. 'Am I?' he said musingly, as they went out to the lift together. 'I wish to God I knew.'

CHAPTER SEVEN

PHILIPPA never forgot that Kabuki performance. The magic of it was all mixed up with the excitement of Matt sitting there beside her. It was being revealed to her more and more plainly that she might make all sorts of good resolutions when he wasn't there, but they dissolved into thin air when he was close, touching her.

Matt had bought a programme in English before they took their seats, but after a glance through it she decided that the plots were too complicated to follow and they seemed to be split up into separate scenes that bore no relation to each other, so very soon she sat back and stopped trying to make sense of it all, and just immersed herself in the visual pleasure of watching the stage.

It was all so different from any play she had ever seen before. The actors wore long, elaborate gowns—gorgeous in red and yellow and blue set off against black or white. The make-up was masklike, thick and white, lips scarlet, eyes darkly emphasised. The acting was suffused with violent passions—love, jealousy, terror, hate, revenge. Everything was larger than life but played with such sustained emotion that it set the senses tingling. The villain's white face was daubed blood-red, and looked so vicious when he threatened the heroine that Philippa found herself clutching Matt's hand as she was carried away by the sheer passion of the performance. The postures were exaggerated, the

135

melodrama full-blooded, and the play gathered a charge of emotion until the tension was almost unbearable. Rivals fought with contained and horrifying violence, lovers parted with sustained anguish.

Between the scenes there were comic turns and dance interludes, and Philippa enjoyed these almost more than the drama itself. The beauty of the dance seemed to be conveyed as much by the flowing lines and dazzling colours of the costumes as by the actual movements of the dancers. They swayed and glided like flowers that had been brought to life in a dream garden, to the music played by traditional plucking, twanging instruments, flutes, percussion.

'I've never seen anything like it, it's fantastic,' Philippa whispered to Matt, her eyes starry, and it all seemed part of an out-of-the-world experience when he slid his arm round her and planted a kiss just above her ear.

'I hope nobody's looking,' he whispered wickedly. 'Such goings-on aren't encouraged in public here!'

She laughed up at him, blue eyes dancing, blissfully happy in this moment when all her dreams of seeing the traditional Japan seemed to be coming true. She quite forgot that not very long ago Adrian Banks had been an important part of her dream. Now Adrian belonged to another life.

The audience were loving the show and entering into the spirit of it. The play was clearly an old familiar favourite and they recognised every move in it. They applauded loudly when the hero appeared along a gangway running across the front of the stage. They hissed the villain and sighed at the sufferings of the heroine, torn from her true love by the machinations of a cruel father.

'Isn't she exquisite?' whispered Philippa as the heroine sank to her knees, her scarlet and white gown flowing round her, her wide tiara glittering against her high-piled black hair.

'She's a he,' Matt whispered back. 'The women's parts are all played by men.'

'No, I don't believe it!' gasped Philippa. That delicate, frail heroine—a man?

She heard Matt's low chuckle. 'Sex equality hasn't caught up with Kabuki yet.'

Philippa ceased to notice the passing of time. It might have been one hour or three when Matt finally suggested they should go out into the foyer for a drink or a snack. The audience seemed to come and go whenever they felt like it, and the foyer was crowded, mostly with middle-aged people, the women soberly dressed in their kimonos of grey or black or brown.

'Some of them have probably been here since eleven o'clock this morning,' said Matt. 'They come in from outlying places and make a day of it.' He took Philippa's empty cup and put it down. 'Saying which, I think we should be getting along. There's another busy day tomorrow.'

'I suppose so,' she sighed. 'I've really enjoyed it—it was wonderful. Thank you for bringing me.'

They strolled back to the hotel along the margin of a park, the lights from the traffic whitening the trees and bushes nearby so that the paths leading further into the depths of the park looked like dark mysterious caves. As they walked they discussed the theatre in a lazy, desultory way, Matt's arm casually round Philippa's shoulder. She had drunk more than one

cup of the rice wine called *sake*, and felt as if she were
floating on the warm air that hardly stirred the tops
of the trees. She had never felt so happy, so carefree
in her whole life. She had no thought for what lay
ahead. Only this magical moment was real. She
wanted it never to end, and when Matt drew her into
the shadow of the trees and took her in his arms she
went willingly, eagerly, as if it were the most natural
thing in the world.

He kissed her gently, his lips tracing the line of
hers, his hand moving on her spine under the lacy
white shawl that she wore over her dress. The touch
of his fingers sent thrill after thrill racing along her
nerves and she clung to him almost desperately as the
kiss deepened and his arm drew her into a closer,
more intimate contact. Then his mouth left hers and
buried itself in the warm hollow of her neck and she
pressed her body yearningly against the length of his
as if she couldn't get close enough. The pleasure that
stirred deep inside her was almost pain. When, at
last, Matt released her she felt like weeping and her
legs sagged under her so that she had to clutch his
arm to steady herself.

'Let's go up to our pad, shall we?' he muttered
thickly, and she could hear the tension in him that
was almost ready to snap, and felt the same tension in
herself. She knew she wouldn't—couldn't—hold
back now. What she felt for Matthew Vane was more
than sex, it was a yearning towards him of her whole
being, body and mind and spirit. It was frightening
and overwhelming.

Entering the hotel lounge, with its Western fur-
nishing and atmosphere, was a shock, like going into
another world.

'I suppose we'd better think about eating,' Matt suggested. 'We've lived on snacks ever since breakfast. Shall we——' He broke off. 'Good lord, look who's here!'

At a table near the entrance to the lounge, sat Sam and Rex. Sam's eyes were fixed on the door. Rex's head was bowed; he was shrivelled up in his chair, his hands clenched together, fingers twisting and untwisting.

Sam saw them come in and was on his feet immediately, walking rapidly across the lounge to them. 'It's Rex,' he said hurriedly, in answer to Matt's raised eyebrows. 'He phoned the nursing-home in Leamington and his mum's pretty bad. Seems she had a heart attack in the night. He's fretting because he can't get to her. Thinks a lot of his mum, Rex does.' Sam took off his glasses and polished them on his handkerchief. 'I didn't suppose anything could be done tonight, but I thought I'd better let you know the position, so I brought him along here with me. He didn't want to stay alone—he's quite lost in Japan. Like a kid.'

'Oh, poor Rex, how wretched for him!' Philippa went quickly across to the table and touched Rex's arm. 'I'm so sorry, Rex,' she said softly, slipping into the seat beside him. Even a word of sympathy helped, she remembered, thinking of the bad time when Gran had her heart attack.

Rex raised a haggard face and he must have seen the real concern in hers. 'Thanks, Pippa, it's hell,' he muttered. 'My mum means a lot to me, always has. She's the only——' He stopped, his mouth working, and Philippa squeezed his hand hard.

Matt and Sam came over to the table. 'Bad luck,

old chap,' Matt said. 'It's a rotten break for you. We've been thinking what can be done to help. Main thing seems to be to try to get you back home as soon as possible. How would you feel about coming along with me to the airport now—it's too late to contact agents—and I'll see if there's anything I can arrange? It might be possible to get a seat on a night flight, or very early in the morning.'

Rex got to his feet; it was as if hope had suddenly pumped some energy into him. 'Oh yes, yes,' he stammered. 'Thank you. If only I could get back home——'

'Right, then.' Matt was his usual masterful self now. Philippa, looking at the strong, controlled face, knew that the moment of weakness just now in the darkness of the park might never have happened. He had put it behind him with the greatest of ease. 'I'll leave you to look after Philippa, Sam. She needs something to eat. I can't say what time I'll be back, so you'll have to play it by ear. I'd suggest getting a night's sleep, both of you, there's nothing you can do.'

He might have been handing out instructions at a staff meeting, Philippa thought, half envious of the way that some men seem to be able to live in two separate parts of themselves, never allowing their emotions to interfere with the practical details of their lives. Gerald had been like that. Probably Sam was, to a lesser extent. Poor old Rex, on the other hand, was very different. Rex was all mixed up. It was sad, but it seemed likely that Rex would be one of life's losers.

'Well,' said Sam, lowering himself into a chair again while Philippa stood watching until Matt and

Rex had disappeared through the lounge doorway, 'this is a turn-up for the book. Rex has been half out of his mind all evening, poor devil. I couldn't think what to do, I tried phoning Matt here, but of course you were out at the theatre. So I thought the best thing was to trundle along and wait until you came in. I knew Matt would be able to take charge of things. He doesn't lose his cool.'

Philippa nodded and sat down beside him. 'No,' she agreed, 'he doesn't.' She wondered how far he had lost his cool out there in the park under the trees. Perhaps it had all been calculated, a run-up to the final inevitable end to the evening. Was he feeling as churned up and frustrated as she was feeling right now? No, of course he wasn't, don't kid yourself, Philippa. Think of all the girl friends he's had. One more or less wouldn't make much difference.

She turned her attention to what Sam was saying, '——a bit in the dark about why Adrian decided to bring Rex and me out here in the first place. We don't seem to have done much except wander round the exhibition. Interesting, of course, but we could probably have gathered most of the information from the new trade journals.' He shook his head puzzledly. 'I suppose you and Matt have been doing the important part—business meetings with top bods and so on?'

'Oh yes, lots of meetings,' Philippa said vaguely, and the doubts raised their nagging little heads again. But she couldn't talk to Sam about her misgivings, about Adrian's suspicions, about the whole baffling set-up of the trip.

'Well, I dare say I'll learn something more inter-esting tomorrow. I was talking to our American

chums after you and Matt left this afternoon and it
seems that they're booked for this trip tomorrow too,
round the Yamaga plant.'

'Yamaga? The people who do all those new
robotics?'

'The same. Should be quite exciting. Our own
robotics are coming along pretty well—that new
program I'm working on back at home has some
pretty far-out ideas. It'll be interesting to see if our
competitors are even further out. Now how about us
toddling along and finding something to eat, Pippa?'

She wondeed if love took your appetite away.
Certainly she didn't feel particularly hungry, but it
would pass the empty time until Matt came back.

'O.K.,' she said. 'Let's go.'

They strolled through the streets, mingling with
the crowds that never seemed to grow any less, and
ate chicken grilled on skewers at an open street-stall,
and wandered along the Ginza with its dazzling neon
lights, and looked at the photographs outside the
night-clubs, and Philippa tried not to mind too much
that it was Sam walking beside her and not Matt. He
was obviously fascinated by everything and she tried
to sound enthusiastic too, but finally she had to
admit that she was asleep on her feet and Sam was
contrite and took her back to the hotel.

'Matt'll be in touch with me, I guess,' he said as
they stood in the entrance foyer. 'I hope he's
managed to fix something for Rex. That bloke
bothers me—Rex, I mean.' He shook his head. 'I get
on pretty well with folk usually, but I've never been
able to make Rex out. Oh well, it takes all sorts——'

They said good night and Philippa took the lift up
to the twentieth floor. Of course Matt wasn't back

yet and without him the suite seemed empty and silent. The big bed looked enormous. If Matt were here now, if Rex's mother hadn't been ill, if Matt hadn't gone off to the airport with him—if—if—if——

She knew the answer to all that. They would be together on that bed now, finishing something that had started under the dark trees in the park. She tried to persuade herself that it was better like this, that she had been saved from making a stupid mistake, but logic had finally ceased to convince. She shivered as she admitted how desperately she wanted Matt. Nothing else mattered, not the past or the future. She ached to be held in his arms.

She must try to be sensible. He couldn't possibly be back for hours, so it was no good sitting and waiting. She brewed a pot of tea, got into bed and finished reading the thriller she had started in the plane. She hadn't guessed right about the murderer, she hardly ever did. As she closed the book she thought wryly that Adrian had picked the wrong person when he had asked her to keep an eye on Matt. She wasn't much good as a detective. And at that moment the whole idea of Matt being engaged in some dark industrial espionage seemed remote and utterly ridiculous.

She wondered if they had managed to get to the airport yet, and if Rex was going to be able to catch an earlier flight. How kind Matt had been, she thought besottedly. He had seen immediately how upset Rex was, and had done just what was needed to help him. He could easily have uttered a few sympathetic words and done nothing at all, and Rex would have had to wait and worry himself sick until they all got back together.

Instead Matt had moved in straight away to help. He was positive and admirable, strong and dominant. He took charge effortlessly, in just the right way. He was just simply—wonderful. Thinking about him made her feel warm and soft and dreamy, and the longing for him, stirring inside her, was almost more than she could bear. But at last she drifted off to sleep hugging the thought of Matt. She could find nothing wrong with him and everything right.

But then, of course, she was in love with the man.

She slept uneasily, waking at intervals, listening subconsciously for Matt to return. At some time she heard muffled noises from the next room and saw a rim of light appear round the bedroom door. She switched on the bedside lamp and the travelling clock told her it was ten to five. Her first impulse was to go in to him, to see that he had all he needed, perhaps to make him a hot drink. She sat up in bed, listening. Then the rim of light disappeared; she heard a couple of muffled thuds followed by complete silence. Matt evidently didn't need anything at this moment except sleep.

A soft smile touched Philippa's mouth. She switched off the lamp and sank into a deep contented sleep herself.

She had set her alarm for half-past seven and when she wakened she showered and dressed quickly and went into the sitting-room. Matt was still heavily asleep, his clothes in a pile on the floor. The divan looked too small for his large body, and his feet stuck out over the end, only half covered by the pink, flower-patterned quilt. He lay twisted half on to his face, one arm flung up across the pillow. Philippa sat on the edge of the divan, feeling such a flood of love and tenderness for the sleeping man that she was almost drowned by it. She put out a hand and touched his cheek where the dark stubble of hair was thrusting through.

She should wake him, she knew. He had appointments for this morning and, as he had told her, Japanese businessmen expect punctuality. She hesitated. She could take one of his arms and shake it, she could make a loud noise at his ear. But instead, she leaned forward and planted a kiss on his right eyelid, the one that wasn't buried in the pillow.

Very slowly the eye opened and Matt rolled over on his back. The wretch, he'd heard her come into the room; he'd been awake all the time. The arm above his head came down and held her wrist firmly when she would have jumped up.

'That was nice,' he smiled. 'Now kiss the other one.' He closed both eyes, waiting.

There was no help for it. Tentatively she placed her lips against his left eyelid and then found that somehow they had travelled down the bristly cheek to his mouth. The kiss was hard and thorough and lasted a long time, and it was Philippa who had the strength to pull away this time.

He groaned in protest. 'Hell, I suppose I must get up and dress. What's the time? I ordered breakfast for eight and I must be on my way by half-past.'

'Then you've got just ten minutes to make yourself pretty,' Philippa grinned. 'Get going, Big Boy,' she joked, and as he began to slide out of bed she turned away quickly.

He chuckled. 'Don't be tactful, I'm not shy.'

She turned her back on him firmly and walked across to draw back the curtains. 'No? Well, you must allow me to be.'

'We'll see about that later,' he said darkly, and made for the shower-room. Philippa fumbled with the curtains with unsteady hands. All this was leading inevitably in one direction. They had one more night in Tokyo and tomorrow they would fly back to England. A one-night stand, she thought, her mouth twisting. Well, so be it, she would have something to remember, even if it were only with tears of despair. And perhaps, just perhaps—it might not finish here. Perhaps they would work together up in his flat at the Manor and he would introduce her to Henry, his computer, and——

Stop it, Pippa! she ordered herself quite violently. Don't forget that Heidi woman. The chairman's confidential secretary—she's in Matt's league, you certainly aren't.

Breakfast arrived at eight o'clock promptly, served by a Japanese waiter in a crisp white jacket, who set a table beside the window.

'O.K., yes?' He smiled at her widely when he had finished.

Philippa smiled back. 'Yes, thank you.' The waiter bowed deeply and departed just as Matt strolled in from the bedroom. Fresh from his shower, wearing the required dark business suit and white shirt, with a patterned burgundy tie, he looked so gorgeous that Philippa's breath caught in her throat.

'Breakfast—ah!' He rubbed his hands. But before he sat down at the table he came up behind her and encircled her waist, nuzzling a kiss behind her ear.

'Good morning again, sweetheart. Did you miss me last night?'

She ignored the implication of that and the sudden wild throb of her heart. 'I heard you come in, very late,' she said, sitting down at the table. 'Tell me, how did you get on? Did you manage to get Rex on a plane?'

He took the chair opposite. 'Finally. It was a bit of a hassle. We had to sit around for hours, hoping for a cancellation on the morning flight. Rex was in a terrible state, he almost smoked himself to a cinder, but in the end it worked and I managed to get him a seat on a JAL flight this morning. I left him, if not exactly happy, at least vastly relieved.' His face sobered. 'I can't help feeling sorry for the poor bloke, some people seem to get all the bad breaks.'

'He talked to you? He never confides much in us at the office.'

Matt looked down at his plate and his mouth was faintly cynical. 'Oh yes, he talked. Indeed he did. More coffee?'

He broke a roll in half. 'Plans,' he said. 'I've got to spend most of the day with Mr Kiwada and his buddies. I think the best thing for you will be to join Sam and go round the Yamaga works with him.'

Philippa nodded, trying to hide her disappointment. The last day in Tokyo and Matt was pushing her off on to Sam!

Matt buttered the roll thoughtfully. 'I wonder— how good's your memory, Pippa?'

'Average, I suppose.'

He nodded. 'Good, well, keep your eyes open— you might pick up something of interest. The Yamaga people have put a lot of new robotics into their production recently. I'd like very much to know just how far they've got—you see, they supply the car industry here, just as we do at home.'

'Matt!' Philippa gasped. 'I'm only a computer operator, for goodness' sake. I don't know about the practical side of robotics—although I must admit I find them fascinating when I see them working.'

'There you are, then,' he said with satisfaction. 'You've got a good brain, you might be able to pick up some bits of information. Ask questions—you'll probably have an interpreter—and they'll be more likely to answer them if they're asked by a girl. Give them your lovely smile, Philippa, and they'll be eating out of your hand.'

She laughed back at him. 'I doubt it very much. But I'll see what I can do.' It would be marvellous to earn Matt's praise, to help him.

'Good girl!' He pushed back his chair and stood up. 'I'll give Sam a ring and ask him to come here and collect you. I'll pick you up at around five o'clock at Sam's hotel. O.K.?'

'O.K.,' said Philippa, trying not to look like a child who has just been denied a special treat. 'I'll see you at five, then.'

'Yes—and oh, by the way, you do realise we have to move out of here today, don't you? We only got the suite for two nights, if you remember. Never fear, I'll find somewhere for us to lay our heads. Perhaps you'll pack for both of us and leave our luggage at reception, to collect later. Now, I'll ring Sam, then I'll be away.'

Already, she saw, he was mentally moving ahead to his meetings. She had been consigned very firmly to the background.

As the day progressed Philippa wished that she could consign the thought of Matt to the background. Sam was delighted to have her with him, and the two Americans, Joe and Earl, didn't seem in the least put out to have a girl wished upon them—quite the reverse, in fact. But even while she talked and laughed and joined in their 'shop' talk Matt was there every minute, like a wonderful secret that she was hugging to her. With part of her mind she knew that it was ridiculous to be *so* much in love that nothing else seemed to register, but there was no help for it. It was like falling into deep, deep water when you had forgotten how to swim.

The tour of the Yamaga factory was exhausting. The activity, the noise, the smell of oil on metal, the blinding flashes when the great robots that stretched and clutched and swung gripping tiny rivets in their claws and deposited them in their allotted places with uncanny accuracy made Philippa's head swim as she trailed around with the party after their Japanese guide. There were about ten in the party and it was almost impossible to catch what the guide was saying in his funny English. As for asking questions—hopeless! Sorry, Matt, it's not my memory that's at fault, it's my tiny brain. Perhaps Sam would have picked up something useful to tell Matt.

They came out into the sunshine holding mementoes of the visit—little boxes containing wax models of the company's trade sign—a red dragon. Joe and Earl tucked their boxes away in the pockets of their bush-jackets to take to their girls back home in Detroit. They were going on a coach tour round Tokyo, before ending the night at a performance of

Sumo wrestling, to which Sam had booked to go with them.

'How about a coach tour?' Sam asked Philippa, but she shook her head. 'A nice quiet sit in the park for me.'

'Sounds a good idea,' Sam agreed.

So they said goodbye to the Americans and repaired to a McDonald's for hamburgers and long cool drinks and creamy gâteaux that looked like fairy palaces, and then found their way to a park and sank gratefully into a seat overlooking a lake, where trees hung low over the water and fountains played and the peace was so profound after the noise and heat of the factory that they both dozed off in the sunshine, later strolling back to the hotel to wait for Matt.

He was late. It was well after six o'clock when he finally appeared in the doorway, and stood looking round for them, big and handsome and self-possessed, a man who stood out in the crowd without any effort at all. Philippa's stomach seemed to disappear. It was a most extraordinary feeling, one that she had never experienced before. In fact, this whole business of falling in love was new to her. She had thought she was in love with Gerald, but it was nothing like this. She could bear Gerald out of her sight for days at a time without feeling that the sun had stopped shining. She could see him coming towards her across a room without an almost painful spasm in the depths of her stomach. His voice didn't set chords vibrating in her head. His touch didn't set volts of electricity surging through her body. Gerald! She could hardly remember what he looked like.

Matt saw them and lifted a hand, smiling, and she felt that the whole of her body was smiling back as he came across to them.

Sam was on his feet immediately. 'Hullo, boss. Drink?'

'No, thanks, Sam, just had one.'

'Sam's going to see the Sumo wrestlers tonight,' Philippa put in quickly, just in case Matt should suggest that they all three spend the evening together.

Matt laughed. 'They're great—in more ways than one. Man-mountains whose strength is as the strength of ten.'

Sam looked blank and Philippa murmured, '—because their heart is pure. Tennyson.'

'If you say so,' grinned Sam, blinking from one to the other of them through his spectacles. 'Never did go much for poetry myself.'

The talk pattered on lightheartedly for a few minutes longer. Sam would have begun a report on the Yamaga factory visit, but Matt said, 'We'll have to leave all that for now. Philippa and I must be getting along. We have to move our hotel today and we've got to check in at the new place.' He stood up. 'We'll look out for you on the plane tomorrow, Sam. Can you find your way?'

'No problem, I'm getting wise to the underground system. My pals from the U.S. come to Japan often and they'll see me right. If you don't see me on the plane come and look for me with a sardine-tin-opener—that's how crowded the underground trains are!'

On this jocular note they parted.

'Where are we going?' asked Philippa, when they

had found a taxi and were being driven in true Kamikaze style through the traffic, which hardly seemed to have thinned out at all, although she reckoned that it must be almost the end of the rush-hour. 'Did you find another hotel?' It didn't matter in the least where they were going, just so long as they were together.

'Wait and see,' said Matt mysteriously and slipped an arm round her and drew her close as the inevitable traffic hold-up began. 'I've transferred our luggage. All we have to do is get there—if we ever do.' But he, too, seemed unusually relaxed and content just to sit there and wait.

After a time they turned out of the main street, down a narrow side street, then into another and another. This must be the Tokyo that you didn't normally see unless you went exploring. Philippa looked for evidence of the old, historical Japan, but apart from lanterns hung over the small shops and cafés, and one or two ancient-looking houses, there was nothing that seemed particularly Japanese. Then at last the taxi stopped outside a pair of rough-hewn wooden gates and Matt got out and paid the driver and pushed open the gates to usher Philippa through.

They walked side by side up a short path where flowering cherry trees spread their laden branches. The blossom had begun to fall and the path was thick with its soft pinkish petals.

Philippa had a curious feeling of excited anticipation. Cherry blossom! This, at last, was the true Japan.

'Are we—is this where we're having dinner?' she asked.

'Certainly.' Matt sounded smug. 'Dinner—and breakfast too.'

They turned a corner and Philippa stopped dead in her tracks. Before them was a scene that might have come straight out of one of her books on the traditional Japan. A low wooden house with a verandah overlooking a little landscaped garden with stone, trees, shrubs and even a miniature pool, all laid out with exquisite care and skill. There was a tiny waterfall, a delicate bridge over a rivulet, narrow stone paths that wound between bushes, mysterious and inviting.

Philippa drew in a breath of sheer pleasure. 'It's lovely. You couldn't believe it could exist right in the middle of the city. It's a *ryokan*, isn't it? A Japanese inn?'

Matt smiled at her delighted face. 'Right first time. You really have been doing your homework.'

'And we're actually staying here?'

'Right again. I thought I'd give you a treat for your last night in Japan and I was lucky enough to get a booking here, through the agency. They don't take foreign tourists all that much because of the language difficulty, but I think we'll get by. I spent several months in Osaka last year and I picked up a couple of dozen words. You won't laugh at my efforts, will you?' He hugged her arm, smiling down at her.

'I wouldn't dare,' she told him, her lips twitching. She was dazed with happiness. This was the most wonderful thing that could have happened, to be with Matt in this fascinating place, to be able to share the fun of something so remote from the great Western-style hotel in the city.

'Let's go in, then,' he said.

Their arrival had evidently been noted. In a tiled square hall, a smiling middle-aged woman in a blue kimono waited to greet the newcomers, sitting back on her heels on a patterned rug. She said a few incomprehensible words and bowed low, nearly to the floor. Matt bowed back and Philippa followed suit. She would have to watch how he behaved in these very unfamiliar surroundings, she wouldn't want to disgrace him. She tried to remember all that she had read about staying in a Japanese inn and knew that the first thing to do was to remove your shoes at the entrance, so she pulled off her high-heeled sandals and selected a pair of slippers from the ones laid out.

Matt watched her with amusement as he, too, shed his shoes. 'I thought I should have to brief you on the etiquette, but I see that won't be necessary. Maybe you have a few things to teach me.'

'Maybe.' She threw him an upward glance under her long lashes as their hostess led the way across the hall and opened a small door into their apartment.

It was like walking into a picture from one of her books. A little hall, and then, as the hostess slid back a paper screen, a cool, square room, almost devoid of furniture. A squat table stood in the centre of the room, there were cushions on the floor and a low dressing-table with an oval mirror against one wall. In a corner stood a small television set and that was all.

Philippa said, 'I'm going to show off my knowledge a bit more—this is tatami matting on the floor and one walks on that only in stockinged feet, correct?'

'Correct.' Matt bowed, Japanese-style, as they

both removed their slippers before they entered the room. 'I think I see our hostess beaming approval.'

The woman was certainly beaming. She disappeared and returned almost immediately with two bowls of green tea on a lacquered tray. She said a few words which seemed to Philippa to be asking a question, Matt held up seven fingers and that was evidently all that was needed. With more smiling and bowing the hostess glided away, closing the sliding screen gracefully behind her.

'We crossed that hurdle,' said Matt with satisfaction. 'Dinner will be served at seven—I hope. Well, here we are. Like it?' He had the look of a benevolent uncle who has just presented a longed-for Christmas gift to a favourite niece.

'Love it!' Philippa lifted her tea-bowl. 'I'm even growing to like the local brew of tea. Thank you for pandering to my romantic notions—did you have to go to much trouble to get us here?'

'A fair bit of hassle,' Matt admitted. He put both his hands on her shoulders and looked down into her happy face. 'But it was worth it to see the way you look now. Is there a thank-you for Father Christmas?'

Philippa's cheeks were pink, her eyes dancing. 'I'll pretend I'm six years old again.' She put down her tea-bowl, linked her arms round his neck and hugged him, holding up her mouth in smiling invitation.

They clung together as they kissed and Philippa closed her eyes, and when he parted her lips with his tongue little shivers of delight rippled through her and she pressed herself against him, responding with a sudden wild longing that came on her unexpectedly, feeling his arousal, glorying in it.

'Hey!' He held her away at last, breathing rapidly. 'That was a very precocious six-year-old! I'll have to watch you, my girl. I can't have my kitten growing up.'

'Perhaps it's a sex kitten?' she suggested demurely, and twisted out of his grasp as he would have pulled her close again. She had never indulged in this kind of foolery. It was fun, made you feel slightly tipsy all the time.

'I shall now,' she announced, 'display all my expert knowledge. She padded across the room to an alcove in the wall. 'This, ladies and gentlemen, is known as a *tokonoma*, in which, as is customary, is hung an *ikebana*. It's rather lovely, isn't it?' She studied the paper scroll hanging in the alcove, delicately painted with a hazy picture of Mount Fuji, its tapering apex rising out of the mist. 'Oh, and this is a *kakemono* and a really super-dooper one too.' Three delicate pink flowers that looked like anemones were arranged in an apparently random fashion in a tall painted vase, the whole thing providing a marvellously satisfying effect.

'There, how did I do?' She turned a laughing face to Matt.

'Full marks for trying,' he said lazily. 'Just one or two slight errors. You got it the wrong way round. 'Scroll—*kakemono*. Flower arrangements—*ikebana*.'

She pulled a face at him. 'Oh well, you can't win 'em all.'

Suddenly he wasn't smiling, and her own smile faltered as she met his dark eyes, fixed on her own. 'You just have to go on trying,' he said very softly.

She drew in a shaky breath and walked across the room to a verandah, overlooking the garden. She leaned on the wooden rail, sure that Matt would come up behind her, sure that his arm would go round her. When it did she rested her head on his shoulder and they stood together looking out over the exquisite garden. A small brown bird fluttered and alighted on the branch of a tree. 'That completes the picture,' Philippa sighed. 'Excellent timing. He must have known the exact moment to arrive.'

'He had his instructions,' Matt said solemnly. 'Everything had to be just right for a romantic young lady.' He kissed her lightly on the tip of her nose and turned her back towards the sitting-room. 'Now,' he said, 'what is expected is that we take our baths before the evening meal is brought in. Most of these *ryokans* still have communal bathrooms, but I took care to find out that this place has its own private ones.' He walked across to the small entrance hall and opened a door leading off it. 'Yes, here we are. Do you know the drill? You sit on this little stool thing and soap yourself first, swill the soap off and then soak in the hot water in this tank-like affair sunk into the floor.' The dark eyes twinkled. 'I'd offer to help, only if I did I'm afraid we'd never get out in time for the meal.'

Philippa pulled a face at him and closed the door.

It would have been rather pleasant, Philippa thought, when she had splashed herself free of soapsuds and they had gurgled down a grid in the floor, to lie down and relax in the hot water, but there was no way she could lie in this steaming tank. Standing upright in a hot bath seemed a very odd thing to do. Soothing, though, when you got the hang of it and let yourself float, treading water as if you were in a swimming-pool. But it was very hot and she must be looking like a boiled lobster already.

She was just climbing out when the door opened and a brown arm appeared round the edge of it. 'I've brought your *yukata*.' A cotton kimono dangled from the end of the brown arm. 'There's another word to add to your list. Like me to dry your back?'

'*No!*' yelled Philippa, grabbing the kimono. 'Go away!'

'Hurry up,' came a plaintive voice. 'I want a bath too, you know.'

Much later, when she remembered that evening, Philippa saw it as a series of clear impressions. All her senses were working overtime. The feel of the soft plump cushions as she knelt at the low table, tucking her feet beside her; the way Matt laughed at his own clumsy attempts to look dignified as he sat cross-legged on a cushion opposite; the smell of the meal served to them in little dishes on trays by the smiling maid, one of which Matt informed her was called *tempura* and tasted deliciously of fried seafood; the heady warmth of the *sake* slipping down her throat, making her whole body glow. Philippa was able to show off her expertise with chopsticks, and the way they laughed together at everything was as if they had known each other for years and not just a few days. The way the inevitable end to the evening lay there between them was like an unspoken promise that made her whole body light and shivery with a sensuous anticipation.

After the meal was cleared away they put on slippers and walked down the verandah steps to admire each feature of the tiny garden. Other guests were out in the garden too, and passed like shadows in the dusk, bowing politely as they went by. Conversation was hushed and the sounds of the city seemed far away. Philippa and Matt walked closely together, both in their cotton kimonos, along the narrow paths.

The smell of damp earth, of mosses clinging to the ancient stones, and ferns that looked as if they had been growing there for hundreds of years, was all around them. A chill arose and Philippa shivered. Matt touched her cheek with his fingers. 'You're getting cold, sweetheart, let's go in.'

'Yes,' she whispered. 'Let's go in.'

In the sitting-room the maid had pushed the table against a wall and on the *tatami* mats were spread mattresses, eiderdowns in covers, and small pillows. A lamp glowed with a yellowish light in a corner of the room.

Matt drew the screens across to close off the verandah from the outside. 'It looks cosy in here.'

Philippa was suddenly overcome by a terrible shyness. 'Yes,' she murmured, looking anywhere but at the two mattresses spread on the *tatami* floor.

But Matt was looking at them. In fact he leaned down and prodded one. 'Nice and soft,' he said, smiling up at her over his shoulder. '*Futon*—there's another word for your vocabulary.'

He straightened up, and in the lamplight she saw that he wasn't smiling any more. Slowly and deliberately he eased the kimono from her shoulders and let it drop on the floor, and she heard his quick intake of breath as he saw that she had discarded everything underneath it.

'You're so beautiful.' His voice was low and husky

as his eyes roamed over her body, smooth and creamy in the lamplight. 'I love you, and I want you so much that it hurts.'

He pulled off his own kimono and drew her down on to the soft mattress, and she went willingly, all shyness gone as she felt his hands on her body, his legs twining with hers as if he could bind her more closely to him. His mouth engulfed hers as they moved together with a rhythm that seemed natural and wonderful. All her body was throbbing as the tide of passion rose for both of them. Matt lifted himself on his hands, looking down at her in the light from the lamp, her coppery hair tumbled on the pillow, her eyes wide, her cheeks flushed. 'I told you, didn't I,' he muttered. 'In the end the arrow shoots itself.'

She didn't know what he was talking about and she didn't care. And those were the last coherent words he spoke for a long time as she reached to his hips and drew him down on her.

She had known that he would be a wonderful lover, and he was. His hands were firm yet gentle on her skin, stroking, moulding, his fingers seeking out the erotic places until she was whimpering for release, moaning his name over and over, her hands exploring his wide back, his shoulders, his strong thighs, as if she were learning every part of him so that she would never forget this magical moment. Shafts of delight passed through her as their passion fused and finally exploded while she clung to him, her fingers digging into the damp firm flesh of his waist.

'Darling—darling——' The words were dragged out of him painfully and she moaned his name again and again.

Then it was over and they lay still, exhausted,

entwined, hearts thudding against each other, until at last Matt rolled away, still holding her. Fumbling at the eiderdown with his free hand, he pulled it over both of them, then slumped back with a huge sigh of content, and in less than a minute she knew he was asleep.

Philippa wriggled herself luxuriously into the curve of his body and his arm was heavy across her as she, too, slept.

CHAPTER EIGHT

PHILIPPA opened her eyes to see the sunlight filtering through the paper screen of the verandah. She turned over and Matt was awake, lying watching her.

'Good morning, my love. Sleep well?' He smiled lazily, black eyes glinting behind long thick lashes, and a wave of warm sensual love washed over her.

It was wonderful, waking to such happiness. It might have been an anti-climax, but it wasn't. If Matt had intended last night to be a one-off thing he showed no sign of it.

'Um—marvellously. These *futon* things are comfy. It's rather fun having a worm's eye view of everything from here. Gives you a different perspective of the world.'

He rubbed his bristly chin against her cheek. 'The world,' he said, 'is a wonderful place this morning. I may break into song at any moment.' His arm went across her and she snuggled up to him luxuriously, loving the smooth warmth of his skin, the chest hairs that tickled her cheek.

'Pippa——'

Suddenly he wasn't joking any longer. They were kissing hungrily, both of them at the same moment awakened to a desperate need that had to be satisfied.

'Quickly—quickly——' he moaned. 'Oh, God, darling, that's heaven, that's wonderful!'

'Wonderful.' Philippa was sobbing under her breath, her fingers digging into his back. Moments—eternity—time stopped for her. Then the shattering fulfilment as she was borne up on a great swooshing wave and down again the other side to lie gasping, her heart thudding in heavy lunging beats.

Beside her, Matt's hard breathing slowly quietened. Then he drew in a long sigh. 'One thing I don't know,' he said huskily, 'is when they bring in breakfast in these places. Damn nuisance.'

With a groan he tore himself away from her and rolled off the mattress. He tossed over the *yukata* she had been wearing last evening. 'I'll go and have a sluice down. Better cover up with that before I get back or I won't be responsible for the consequences! I find you quite impossible to resist, my dearest girl.'

Philippa lay and watched him as he padded across the room to the bathroom off the little entrance hall, and her heart squeezed up with love for him. His body was beautiful, so strong and lean and lithe, and he moved with a kind of lilt in his step, as if life were something to be enjoyed. God, but she loved him.

And he loved her, that was what was so wonderful. He had said it last night. He had said, 'I love you,' quite clearly, she was sure of it. He must have meant it—there wasn't any need to say it if he hadn't was there? It couldn't have been merely his way of persuading her to make love with him, could it? Heaven knows, she hadn't needed any persuading, she thought, and her cheeks began to burn at the memory of last night.

It had been so perfect that it couldn't just end here. What had started between them would surely go on. She didn't dare ask herself how it would go on, or how long it would last, but she was certain that last night wasn't the end. They would see each other when they got back, perhaps work together as he'd suggested. And before that there was the long flight home. It would be so different from the flight out here. They could talk to each other now, they were friends and lovers; Matt might even tell her about the business meetings he had had. But if he didn't—if it was all still confidential—she would understand and not feel left out.

The trip to Tokyo, which had started so badly, was ending on a high note, and the homeward flight, when they boarded the plane later in the day, confirmed it in Philippa's bemused mind. Matt was a different person from the silent, ironic individual she had started out with from Warwick, only days before. And it wasn't just because last night they had made love, she assured herself. Ever since yesterday morning, after he had got in so late from taking Rex to the airport, he had been different—easier, more friendly, not suddenly changing his mood so that she felt he was pushing her away.

Travelling east they were flying away from the sun and it seemed wrong, somehow, that they should be flying towards the darkness, and not the other way round, but even the darkness had its compensations There was a cosy feeling about the shaded, comfortable cabin, where the first-class seats were only half full. Matt talked a little—about Japan and his previous visits there, telling her about all the sights that there had been no time to see, the temples and castles and lakes and gardens. 'We'll have to go back some time,' he said, 'and I'll show you the rest.'

We! Philippa hugged that little word to her.

'Meanwhile,' he went on, 'tell me about yourself, Pippa. It seems ridiculous, but I don't know a thing about you—somehow there hasn't been the opportunity to talk.'

Her defences were down. The very fact that he wanted to know about her was enough to make her open up. She found herself telling him about her father, whom she had loved, and who had walked out when she was ten and never come back. And about her pretty mother who, after a divorce, had married again and gone off to South Africa with hardly a backward look. 'You could come out to us when you've finished with school, darling,' she'd said vaguely. 'You wouldn't want to leave all your friends now, would you? And Gran will look after you.'

'So you lived with your grandmother—your mother's mother?' Matt put in. 'You were happy with her?'

'She was wonderful and I loved her dearly. She died only a few months ago.'

He nodded. 'Tough,' he said. 'I know. I had a beloved grandmother.'

There was a long silence, then he said, 'This fellow—the one you wouldn't tell me about?'

Philippa said, 'Not much to tell. I thought I was in love with him. He asked me to marry him.' Her voice tightened as she added, 'He just forgot to mention that he had a wife already.'

Matt muttered something under his breath. Then he said, 'You haven't had much luck, my poor Pippa. We must see about changing all that.'

We again! She began to let herself believe that he really meant them to be together. It would be great if she was the kind of girl who could ask him, if she could say casually, 'What have you got in mind for us?' But she wasn't that kind of girl and she couldn't, and that was that.

The time passed. Meals appeared at intervals. A Western film took up an hour or so. Matt had bought three of Philippa's favourite detective stories at the airport and she read them on and off, but she couldn't concentrate; she was so drowned in the heady exhilaration of loving and being loved that all she needed to do was snuggle down beside Matt and let dreams take over. She had never thought of herself as a romantic, but Matt said she was, so she must be.

Matt got out his briefcase and spread papers on the table before him, but he, for once, seemed to have little zest for business, and finally he packed them away.

'All tied up?' murmured Philippa. Matt had been cagey about his business meetings before, but everything was different now.

'What isn't can wait till I get back to the office.' He hoisted his case into the overhead locker.

She yawned. She was beginning to feel deliciously sleepy again and the atmosphere in the cabin was distinctly drowsy. 'Was it all worth it? Did the trip go as you wanted?'

'Everything was fine. Better than I'd hoped or expected. Some day I'll tell you the whole story,' he added enigmatically. 'But not now.'

Lights were lowered to a glimmer. Seats were tipped back and a stewardess, thoughtful as ever for their comfort, brought fleecy rugs to cover their knees.

'I'd like that,' Philippa murmured. He trusted her now, he wouldn't push her away again. Her hand sought his under the run and was held in his big hand. He leaned over and kissed her lingeringly. 'I love you, Pippa,' he said against her lips.

'And I love you, darling Matt, so very much,' she whispered back. Sighing, cocooned in warmth and love, she laid back her head and drifted off into a blissful sleep.

Somewhere over Europe it began to get light and the plane finally touched down at Heathrow early on a cold April morning. Philippa shivered in her thin suit as they finally got through Customs. They had contacted Sam on the journey and they all walked up to the arrivals lounge together.

The company chauffeur was waiting for them. 'Good trip, sir? A message came through for you from Head Office.' He handed Matt an envelope, nodded to Sam and Philippa and held out his hand for Philippa's bag.

Matt's face was expressionless as he ripped open the envelope and glanced at the note inside. He pushed the slip of paper back into its envelope and stuck it in an inside pocket.

'Excellent trip, thanks, Bob. You've managed to park the car?'

As they made their way up escalators, along passages, to the car-park he shot out orders. 'We'll make straight for Warwick and drop Miss Marsden off, Bob. Then I want to get to Head Office as soon as possible. I'd like you to come along with me, Sam.'

Philippa sensed the change in him and, for a moment, felt herself give way to panic. He had sounded almost as if he wanted to get rid of her as quickly as possible. Then she pulled herself together. She mustn't be touchy; of course she couldn't expect him to devote his attention to her now that they were back in England. He would be immersed in business—at least for a while. But when he got in the front of the car beside the chauffeur, leaving her to sit with Sam at the back, it was as if a cold breeze had blown over her.

The M1 was congested and as the powerful car ate up the miles conversation was limited. Matt turned back now and again with some general remark, but he seemed detached and preoccupied, and finally he sat silent, apparently lost in thought.

When the car pulled up outside Mrs Smithson's house in Warwick that good lady, who had evidently been at the window, hurried out of the front door and down the short path.

'So here you are,' she beamed. 'What a mercy to see you back safe and sound after all these hijacks and terrible things that go on!' She kissed Philippa. 'Now do come in, Mr Vane, and have a nice cup of coffee. And ask your driver and the other gentleman too.' She glanced doubtfully towards the car where Sam and the chauffeur were sitting.

'It's most kind of you, but I'm afraid I have to get on.' Matt was already back at the car, having deposited Philippa's bag at the front door. He nodded to Mrs Smithson and with a brisk, 'See you soon, Philippa. Take the rest of the day off,' he climbed in and saluted briefly as the car reversed and purred away down the street.

Mrs Smithson looked disappointed. 'Well, what a pity he couldn't stay. But come in, dear, and tell me all about it. Have you had a lovely time? I can't wait to hear.' She bustled off towards the kitchen.

Philippa followed slowly. 'Lovely,' she said, and

then, pushing away a small black cloud of depression that was hovering over her, 'Absolutely lovely,' she added firmly. 'I've brought you a small present from Tokyo,' and she handed over a parcel containing the little purse she had bought in the hotel shopping complex.

'My dear, you shouldn't have! Oh, it's beautiful—thank you.' Mrs Smithson took the purse from its wrappings and crooned over it with delight. Then she placed it carefully on the table and stood back, admiring it.

The little purse was made of stiff black silk and closely embroidered in a flower pattern with gossamer-like threads of blue and green and gold. It was exquisite, like everything in the craft shop at the hotel. Seeing it there on the kitchen table brought everything back so vividly that Philippa suddenly wanted to cry. It was all over, and she could hardly believe, now, that it had happened.

Mrs Smithson put the coffee-mugs on the table. 'You'll like a rest now, dear, after that long journey. Have a nice lie down on your bed. Mr Vane said to take the rest of the day off.'

She couldn't bear the kindly, motherly tone in Mrs Smithson's voice, or the idea of a nice lie down on her bed. She had to be up and doing.

'I'm not a bit tired,' she said brightly. 'I had a good sleep on the plane.' With my hand in Matt's, she thought, and swallowed hard. 'I'll go and pick up my car from the garage and then I'll drive over to the office. The sooner I get back into harness the better.' She finished her coffee and put down the mug. 'I'll tell you all about Tokyo when I get home later on.'

*   *   *

'And how was the mysterious Orient? Did you have a super time?' Mona Drew, from the general office, must have seen Philippa come in, for she had followed her upstairs with the excuse of offering some fresh-brewed coffee and now sat on the edge of Sam's empty desk, her plump face alight with curiosity. Mona liked to keep tabs on everything that went on in the office.

'Super,' said Philippa mechanically. 'Out of this world.' And before Mona could get around to her usual routine of questions she put one herself. 'How's everything been going on here without us?'

Mona's pale blue eyes looked as if they might pop out. 'You'd never believe! Rumours—comings and goings—visits from the chairman—two plain-clothes fellows snooping round combing through the files. There's been some dirty work going on around here, take it from me, Pippa.' Mona licked her lips with relish. 'Someone here—someone up top—is for the high-jump. That's what everyone's saying.'

'Who?' Philippa had gone icy cold.

Mona shrugged. 'Not many to choose from, are there? You can take your pick. Must go now, we're busy downstairs.' At the door she stopped. 'Oh, by the way, did you know that Rex Hanling's mother had died? Terry Brown's sister works at the nursing-home where she's been since Christmas. Rex was in your party in Tokyo, wasn't he? Apparently he got back just before she died—he was in a terrible state, Terry's sister said.'

Philippa nodded slowly. 'I'm glad he got back in time,' she said.

She sat alone in the office when Mona had gone. Lunchtime came and went and she hardly noticed.

Someone up top is for the high-jump. Mona's words went over and over in her mind like a stuck gramophone record. 'I don't believe it,' she said aloud. 'He couldn't—he wouldn't—he's not like that.'

Then she remembered how she had said those very words before, when someone had told her that Gerald was married.

Without Sam and Rex the little office seemed like a morgue. She switched on her computer and stuck in the disk and called up the program she'd been working on before they left for Tokyo, but it didn't mean a thing. Better not mess about with it, she would only foul it up permanently if she did. She switched off again and sat staring at the blank screen, feeling like death. What was happening at Head Office in Birmingham? What had been in that message that had been awaiting Matt at Heathrow? If only there were someone she could ask, something she could do, but there was nothing.

Sam came into the office halfway through the afternoon, by which time Philippa was nearly screaming with nerves. He grinned palely at her and sank into his chair. 'God, I'm creased! You don't need a bloody inquisition at the end of a fifteen-hour flight. Any tea going?'

'I've just made some.' Philippa poured him a cup and sat waiting, her nails biting into her palms.

'Why the summons to Head Office?' she ventured, when she couldn't bear the silence any longer. 'What did they want?'

Sam's eyes narrowed behind his spectacles. 'Evidence, that's what they wanted.' She had never seen the pleasant, easy-going Sam look so grim.

He took a gulp of tea. 'Nasty business, Pippa. It always is when someone you've worked with turns out to be crooked.'

'Sam—*who*?' she croaked. Her palms were damp; her mouth was like sandpaper.

He looked with surprise at her. 'Rex, of course. Rex Hanling, the bloody fool. And Adrian Banks—he's the master-mind, but somehow it seems worse that Rex—what's the matter, Pippa, are you all right?'

The office was spinning round and round. She felt Sam's hand on her neck, pushing her head down. When the dizziness had passed she lifted her head and Sam was kneeling in front of her, his face pale.

'You scared me,' he said worriedly. 'What happened?'

She blinked stupidly. 'I don't know. Shock, I suppose, on top of the jet-lag.' She looked over towards Rex's empty chair. 'I can't believe—oh, it's horrid, isn't it?'

Sam nodded glumly and got to his feet. 'Beastly business about Rex. Although I wasn't altogether surprised about Adrian Banks. I never——' He stopped. 'Sorry, Pippa. I forgot you and Banks——'

Philippa shook her head. 'It was never anything much, Sam.' Adrian! she thought. I never guessed. All that business about watching Matt—he must have been scared that she would somehow find out the game he was playing and had tried to put her off the scent by incriminating Matt.

Adrian—Rex—Matt—— She couldn't sort it out yet. She didn't want to talk to Sam about it; she didn't want to know anything about the scandal that would soon break over the office. There was only one thing that filled her mind. 'Did Matt come back with you?' she asked Sam.

'No, he's still in Birmingham. There's a lot to sort out. Oh lord, I nearly forgot!' He clapped a hand to his forehead. 'He asked me to give you a message if you were in the office.'

Philippa drew in a quick breath. 'Yes?'

'Just to say that he'll be held up for a day or two, but he'll be in touch about the work you were going to do for him.'

She felt her cheeks begin to burn. 'Oh yes, thanks, Sam. Just some programming he asked me to try my hand at. He's planning a hi-tech installation in his flat.' He hadn't forgotten her—not even in the middle of the all the turmoil that must be going on at Head Office. Oh, Matt—darling, darling——

'That'll be good practice for you.' Sam didn't seem unduly interested, and that was a relief. 'Well, I suppose I'd better get back into harness. Work goes on in spite of all the spills and thrills. How do you feel about it, Pippa? Would you like to take over where Rex left off, or aren't you up to it? Get along home if you like, another half-day won't make any difference.'

'No, I'd like to get started,' Philippa said hastily. So long as she was still in the office there was a chance of seeing Matt, however remote.

But it was three dreary days before she saw him again. The weekend went on for eternity. Philippa had to be very stern with herself to make herself go out and not stay within earshot of the telephone. So far as she knew Matt hadn't got her telephone number, but if he really wanted to get in touch he could surely find it.

But he didn't ring. She cleaned her room on Saturday morning, went to the badminton club in the afternoon and looked at television with the Smithsons in the evening. On Sunday she walked across the fields, nearly to Kenilworth, to tire herself out. In the evening she washed her hair and did her nails and went to bed early. Surely tomorrow she would hear something of Matt.

The whole office was buzzing with rumours on Monday. Philippa kept to her own office and worked like mad, under Sam's guidance. She hadn't before done any programming at this level and at least it kept her mind fully occupied. The girls had a common-room to themselves and Philippa usually took her lunch in there, but today she ate her sandwiches in her own office with Sam. As the afternoon wore on her head began to ache and the office got fuggy and the symbols on the VDU screen began to dance before her eyes.

At half-past five the telephone rang. Sam answered it and passed the receiver over to Philippa. 'For you, Pippa. It's the boss,' he mouthed silently.

Her heart was thumping like mad. 'Hullo,' she forced through dry lips.

'Hullo, Pippa, how are you?' His voice on the phone was just the same and her knees went weak. She groped for a chair and sank into it. 'Oh, I'm fine.' She swallowed, casting a sideways glance at Sam on the other side of the office. 'Working hard. Sam's putting me through the mill.'

She heard his laugh and her fingers relaxed on the receiver. If he could laugh like that then everything was all right. 'That's what I like to hear,' he said. Then, 'How are you fixed for this evening? Could we get together and I'll introduce you to Henry?'

'Henry?' Oh *no*, she didn't think she could bear a threesome.

'Yes, Henry—my computer—don't you remember?'

'Oh, of course, how silly of me,' she jabbered. 'Yes, I'd like that.'

'Good.' Matt sounded satisfied. 'There are a few things I want to talk over with you, too. Things have been pretty fraught here, but we've nearly cleared up now and there isn't much else I can do for the moment. You've heard, of course?'

'Of course.'

There was a short silence. Then he said, 'How about if you go up to the flat when you've finished work and wait there for me and I'll be along as soon as I can get away. I'll ring Robbins and tell him to leave the flat door unlocked.' Robbins was the caretaker. 'Is that O.K. with you?'

'Yes,' she said. 'I'll wait for you.' I'd wait for you all the rest of my life, she thought soberly, and it was like making a vow.

Sam eyed her flushed cheeks thoughtfully. 'Can you work on till six, Pippa, or do you want to get away?'

'Oh no—I mean yes, I can work till six.'

It was after six by the time Sam called a halt. 'You're doing great, Pippa,' he said. 'How would you like Rex's job? It would be a step up for you. Think about it and if you're keen I'll put in a word for you.'

She stared at him uncertainly. Last week she would have jumped at the offer. 'Oh—oh, thank you, Sam, that's very good of you.'

'Let me know tomorrow,' said Sam in his practical way. 'Ready? We'll lock up, then.'

In the girls' room Philippa washed her face and reapplied make-up with shaking hands. She untied the ribbon that held back her shining coppery hair and let it curve round her face and fall to her shoulders. She took the little polar-bear brooch that Matt had given her in Anchorage out of her handbag and pinned it on to her blouse. It seemed like a talisman.

Her heart was pounding away as she climbed the narrow staircase to the penthouse flat. Outside the oak door she hesitated, looking at her watch. He couldn't be here yet, not with all the rush-hour traffic in Birmingham and he'd said, 'Go up to the flat and wait for me.'

The door was unlocked. She pushed it open and walked across the hall to the long, elegant living-room. The room was shadowy in the dusk and she put her hand round the door and switched on the light.

On a squashy pale-leather sofa, her white fur jacket tossed nonchalantly over the back of it, lounged a blonde girl in a black tailored suit. She looked very much at home. Philippa's knees started to tremble. Heidi Jones—the girl who had been with Matt that night at the Warwick Hotel. The chairman's P.A. Adrian's words echoed sickeningly in her head: 'She and Matt Vane have a big thing going.' Oh God, how could she have forgotten?

'Hullo, you've come, then.' Curious green eyes raked Philippa from head to foot. 'Come and sit down—er—Philippa, is it?' Her voice was light, with the faintest of foreign inflections.

Philippa sank into a deep chair opposite—not because she wanted to but because she was afraid that her legs wouldn't support her any longer. Something in the way the other girl was staring at her made her blood curdle.

'Matt told me he was seeing you up here this evening.' The thin lips smiled but the light green eyes held malice. 'I knew he was going to find it difficult to tell you what he needed to say, poor lamb, so I thought I'd come along first and do the spadework for him.'

Philippa passed her tongue over dry lips. 'What are you talking about?'

Again the thin smile. 'Better get it said quickly, my dear. You may feel a little hurt, but I'm sure you'll be sensible about it. You see, I know how Matt operates.' She ran a finger along a pleat in her smooth black skirt. 'He can be very—thoughtless about other people's feelings when he has unpleasant business matters to attend to.'

'I really don't——'

'Just be quiet and listen,' the girl snapped, not troubling now to hide her contempt. 'Matt took you to Tokyo because he had to find out whether you were the one who was passing confidential information to Adrian Banks. He knew it was one of the three of you in your department and you seemed the most likely, as you were having an affair with the Banks man. As it happens, you weren't involved, but presumably Matt went his own way about investigating you.' The thin lips drew into a sneer. 'You're quite an attractive child, I've no doubt he didn't find it difficult or unrewarding.'

It wasn't happening; she was having a nightmare.

She wanted to scream herself awake, but no sound would come. She stared into the pale green eyes of the woman on the sofa and couldn't say a word.

Heidi Jones leaned forward and patted her arm. 'It's been a shock, my dear, but you'll soon get over it. Matt seemed rather upset that he'd given you a raw deal. He'll be coming along himself shortly to explain things to you and I know you'll be sensible about it—I told him so.' She laughed lightly. 'We women have to expect our men to be—well, somewhat insensitive. We have to put up with it. I've known Matt a long time and I understand him very well, but I still don't expect him to see everything my way.'

She uncoiled herself and got to her feet. 'Now, I'll leave you to see him and sort things out. I'm on my way to meet some friends in Stratford and Matt will be joining us later.' She picked up the fur jacket, slung it round her shoulders, and with a casual wave of a white hand she drifted across the room and closed the door behind her.

Philippa sat very still for a time. Then she got up and walked stiffly to the window and opened it, breathing in the clean country air and letting out the cloying perfume that hung about the room.

Of course. It all hung together now. There was no way she could disbelieve Heidi Jones. As the Chairman's personal assistant there wouldn't be much she didn't know about what went on at high levels.

Yes, she knew everything. She knew that Matt was coming here, that Philippa would be waiting for him. She knew all about the Tokyo trip—and what she didn't know she had evidently guessed pretty accurately. He had talked about it to her—perhaps they had laughed together. 'It was pathetically simple,' he would have said. 'The poor girl was a pushover. A nice kid, I felt rather a heel. I was quite glad to find she wasn't involved with Banks and his dirty work.'

Philippa leaned from the window, looking down. It would be so easy—just a sickening moment and then the concrete path below would blot out everything. But she wasn't that kind of girl. She was a sensible girl, as the revolting Heidi woman had said, not the kind to make melodramatic gestures. Sensible! Oh yes, a sensible girl, trained in logic. Except that she happened to be a very poor judge of men, which was just too bad, wasn't it? Gerald had deceived her and hurt her badly. Adrian had turned out to be a common-or-garden crook.

And Matt——! Her hand closed round the velvet curtain, clutching it convulsively. She was icy cold and shaking inside and she couldn't possibly face Matt yet. She must get away quickly and give herself time to get control, otherwise she would break down and make a fool of herself. She stumbled across the room and plunged down the short flight of stairs.

'Hey! Where do you think you're going?'

Matt's voice, close to her ear. Matt's arms holding her.

She pulled herself up. 'I—I have to go. Something I forgot,' she mumbled. 'Please let me go—it's—it's important.' She wriggled to pull away, but was held fast at the foot of the stairway.

'Oh no, you don't, my girl! There's nothing more important than what I've got to say to you. Come along up.'

His hand was at her back, propelling her up the stairs and somehow she managed to reach the top. 'Now then,' he said calmly. 'Come and sit down and tell me what all this is about.' He pushed her into a chair and stood looking down at her. 'You look as if you'd encountered another earthquake. We don't have them here, you know.' He walked across the room and came back holding out a glass. 'Drink this. Go on, drink it.'

Philippa took a swig of the brandy and coughed as it caught at her dry throat. But at least the ice was melting inside her. Matt poured himself a drink and came and sat beside her on the sofa, putting out his other arm to draw her towards him.

She edged away. 'Don't touch me!' she blurted out in a strangled voice.

She felt him go rigid. 'Philippa, what is this? I want to know.'

She made herself look at him and the sternness of his face frightened her, but she drew in a shaky breath and said, 'Heidi Jones was here, waiting, when I came up.'

'Yes?' He wasn't surprised. He wasn't going to help her.

She forced herself to go on, intoning the words without expression. 'She said she'd come to break the news to me that you took me to Tokyo with you in order to find out whether I was implicated with Adrian Banks in cheating the company. That you intended to get my confidence. That you would doubtless have your own way of doing it. She—left nothing to the imagination.'

There was a short silence. Then, 'Is that all?' he said.

The ice was creeping back again. 'Is it true?'

'Yes,' he said.

The silence was longer this time. Then, 'I—see,' Philippa said dully. 'Then I'll go now, there really isn't any more to be said.'

Somehow she got to her feet. Somehow she reached the other side of the room, moving like a marionette, every step an agony. It seemed a long, long way.

'Pippa——' Matt's voice halted her as she reached for the doorknob.

He was on his feet, but he didn't come nearer. 'There's one other thing she didn't tell you, because she didn't know.'

Philippa waited numbly.

'She didn't tell you that I fell in love with you.'

Over the length of the room there was a silence and a stillness that settled like something tangible. Very slowly Philippa turned round. If she could see his face she would know, but from this distance, with only the shaded wall-lights, his expression was unreadable.

Hope was stirring in Philippa and yet she couldn't move. She had been so wrong before—so often— could she believe that this was true?'

He spoke her name then, in a deep, shaky voice, so unlike his usual confident one. 'Pippa—*please*, darling.'

He held out his arms to her and she stumbled across the room as if some outside agency had propelled her. His arms closed round her and they clung together, and the tears were streaming down her cheeks. He kissed her eyes, her mouth, her wet cheeks, murmuring words of love that shook her through and through.

'I thought—I thought——' she stammered at last.

'Don't think,' he said, masterful again now. 'This
is no time for thinking. It's been a hellish two days,
my love, wanting you and wanting you and being
tied up in a sordid affair of lies and corruption. I
could hardly keep my mind on what was happening.'

So perhaps she had been wrong about him—
perhaps he wasn't, after all, a man who could live his
life in two separate compartments.

She reached up and put her arms round his neck
and drew his mouth down to hers. 'I'm not thinking
any longer,' she whispered against his lips.

With a whoop of triumph Matt lifted her off her
feet and carried her across the room and into the
bedroom. She saw nothing of the room that later she
would know so intimately, only a wide, shadowy
bed. Her hands shook as she unfastened the buttons
on her blouse, pulled down the zip of her skirt. For
just a second she hesitated, then bra and tights
followed.

Matt was ahead of her, their clothes lay in one
scattered heap on the carpet. In the dim light that
filtered in from the next room he looked at her.
'You're unbelievable, my darling, generous girl,' he
muttered, and very slowly put out a hand and
touched her hair, and drew her against his hard,
warm body. Still entwined, they toppled over on to
the bed and Philippa began to laugh helplessly. Matt
growled, 'See? I can't tear myself away from you.
Want me to show you?'

'Yes,' she whispered. 'Oh yes!' And her laughter
stopped as his mouth closed over hers.

CHAPTER NINE

IT was quite dark when they finally surfaced. 'We'll have a look in the freezer,' said Matt. 'It isn't true that love makes you lose your appetite. I'm famished!'

'Me too,' Philippa admitted. She had been introduced to the flat's super bathroom and was pink and glowing from her shower.

They found a gourmet pack of Scotch salmon in a béchamel sauce, and Philippa heated it in the microwave while Matt had his shower. She thawed raspberries and cut slices of Cornish ice-cream and made coffee in the filter machine.

Matt opened a bottle of wine and they ate in leisurely satisfaction, at peace with their world. Later, they moved to the sofa and Philippa curled up against Matt as they drank their coffee.

'I still can't quite believe it's true,' she murmured. 'It's all happened so quickly.'

'Falling in love takes no time at all.' Matt rested his cheek against her hair. 'It's taken me thirty-two years to learn that great truth.'

She chuckled. 'You're not trying to tell me that you've never fallen in love before?'

He considered that. 'I could say that I've always managed to do a balancing act—never actually fallen. This is quite, quite different. How about you?'

'Quite, quite different,' she echoed solemnly.

There was a silence, each of them following a

different train of thought.

Then Philippa said, 'When did you find out—about Adrian? And Rex?'

He sighed. 'Do you really want to talk about all that?'

'I want to know,' she said flatly, 'so that I can start to forget.'

'Forget Adrian Banks?' he shot out, suddenly angry. 'You weren't—you told me you——'

She stroked his cheek. 'Calm yourself. I can forget Adrian in no time at all. But it might take me a little longer to forget that you suspected me of cheating.'

Matt groaned. 'I didn't know you then. We knew somebody was selling some of our confidential research to some rather shady competitors of ours overseas and for various reasons we suspected it might be Banks. If so, probably someone in your department was helping him—Sam, Rex, or you. You seemed the most likely—it was known that you and Banks were seeing each other.' He looked suddenly angry.

Philippa changed the subject hastily. 'But why the trip to Tokyo?'

'I imagine that was a red herring, to divert attention from the ploys Banks was engaged in on the other side of the world. Tokyo was supposed to be a fact-finding trip. Fortunately it turned out pretty well—I made some good contacts there and something may come of it all later.'

'I still can't see why Adrian should have included me,' Philippa said slowly.

'Two reasons. One, no doubt, was to provide diversion during the stay—I'll leave you to guess how. The other, possibly, to give him a second string to his bow—he'd already got Rex working for him, and it would have been a bonus to have you as well. One thing about crooked operators is their conceit. He would have reckoned on your falling so hard for his fatal charms that you'd be willing to feed him the information he needed. All you would have to do would be to slip him some data codes and he'd do the rest. He was a super-expert, you know, he'd been hacking into some of our newest programs—no trouble at all.'

Philippa gasped. 'He told me he didn't know a thing about computers.'

'Well, he would, wouldn't he? He wouldn't announce his intentions. The fellow was clever—and subtle.'

She digested all that in silence for a time. Then she said, 'And Rex? How did he come into it?'

'That's rather a sad story. Rex Hanling is what they call a fall guy, I'm afraid. Failed marriage, wife badgering him for back payment of maintenance, children at boarding-schools, mother in a private nursing-home. He was skint. He was stupid enough to play the computer game himself—he'd been multiplying his salary cheques by five. Banks found out and was blackmailing him into giving him the info he needed. Very simple really.'

'Poor Rex,' said Philippa softly. 'I always felt rather sorry for him, I don't know why.'

Unexpectedly Matt said, 'I do too. He earned my gratitude that night I took him to the airport in Tokyo. We sat there for ages, waiting, and suddenly he seemed to snap. He told me the whole story—everything we wanted to know. I think the poor devil knew he was going to lose his mother—he seemed to care a lot about her—and if she was gone he wanted to make a clean breast of everything. He said he felt better afterwards.'

'What will happen to him?' asked Philippa.

'It's not decided yet. It's not clear what the legal angle is, but I doubt if we shall prosecute in any case. With Banks it's different, but we'll have to find him first. He's probably in South America by now.'

There was a long silence. Then Philippa said, 'It's all rather horrid. Horrid to think you were suspecting me at first—watching me.'

'Not for very long. A few things made me wonder—you seemed to be acting rather oddly at times—quizzing me.'

Philippa started to laugh and when she had started she couldn't stop. 'It's f-funny——' she gasped. 'You're not going to b-believe this.'

Matt shook her. 'What's the joke? Come on, tell me!'

She groped for a hanky and wiped her eyes. 'While you were watching me I was—' another paroxysm shook her '—*I* was watching *you*.'

He shot upright. 'What?'

'Adrian told me he was sure that you were passing on company secrets to someone in the U.S. He said you'd been working there. He asked me to—' she gurgled again '—to watch you and try and find out if you were up to anything in Japan.'

He stared at her incredulously. 'Good God!'

She nodded. 'Yes, it seems crazy now.' She hesitated, then she said, 'He told me something else too—that you and Heidi Jones were having an affair. Was that another lie? Don't tell me if you don't want to, but she was rather unpleasant to me and I wondered——'

'It was another lie,' he said. 'Heidi Jones is the chairman's P.A. and even if I'd fancied her I wouldn't have—er—fallen in with her suggestion that we should get together. The chairman's a friend of mine and it would have been altogether too complicated. Heidi made the running now and again, we had a few dinners together, but that was all—cross my heart. She's not my type and I never wanted anything more anyway.'

But she did, Philippa thought, and then dismissed Heidi Jones from her mind with satisfaction. If she was waiting for Matt to join her in Stratford then she'd have a long wait.

There was silence in the big quiet room except for the distant rumble of traffic on the main road outside the gates.

'Matt—when did you know?' Philippa asked.

'That I was in love with you?' His fingers stroked her cheek, moved down to her neck. 'I think it was that night of the earth tremor,' he went on, absently unfastening the buttons of her blouse, 'although I didn't realise it then. You were scared stiff, and you turned to me and I held you. I expect it's an out-of-date attitude, but I liked that. I liked the feel of you in my arms, the feeling that I was somehow protecting you. And—well, how do you explain these things?' His hand closed over the soft swell of her breast and she felt a jolt deep inside her. 'The chemistry was right, but it was more, much more, than that.'

'Um, I know.' She pressed closer to him on the wide sofa. 'You can't explain love, you can only feel

it. It's very odd—just one person out of all the world
and no words to say why that person is the only one.'

He reached out and smoothed back her silky
coppery hair with his free hand and his dark eyes,
heavy with desire, looked deep into hers. 'I love you,
Pippa, my darling. You will marry me, won't you? I
need you with me always, to live with, to care for, to
talk to, sometimes to work together, to bear my children. You want children?'

'Oh yes—lots,' she murmured contentedly.

He chuckled softly. 'We'll have to program Henry
to work out the optimum number that my income
will support.'

She pulled away from him. 'Don't you dare bring
Henry into this!'

Matt laughed lazily and drew her back against
him. 'Between you and Henry I know which of you
would always win.'

'I should jolly well hope you do!' she spluttered
indignantly. 'I will allow Henry to have you during
working hours, but he must be kept strictly out of
our private life.'

'I'll tell him,' Matt promised. 'He had that
marvellous idea that he could work out how many
times a married couple should make love. Just now
he seems obsessed by sex.'

They lay back on the sofa in silence. But after a
time the space around them began to quiver with
tension, like a spring being stretched to its limit.

At last Philippa could bear it no longer. 'Matt,' she
said in a small, shaky voice, 'do you really think
Henry can count all that well?'

'To hell with Henry,' he groaned as his arms
closed round her.

Take 4 best-selling love stories FREE
Plus get a FREE surprise gift!

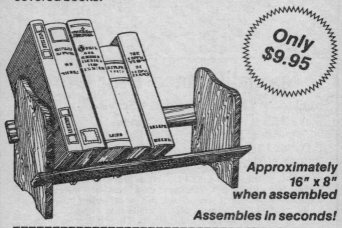

Harlequin Signature Edition

Carole Mortimer

Merlyn's Magic

She came to him from out of the storm and was drawn into
his yearning arms—the tempestuous night held a magic
all its own.

You've enjoyed Carole Mortimer's Harlequin Presents
stories, and her previous bestseller, *Gypsy*.

Now, don't miss her latest, most exciting bestseller,
Merlyn's Magic!

IN JULY

MERMG